USA TODAY BESTSELLING AUTHOR

DALE MAYER

DANGEROUS DESIGNS

BOOK 1 OF THE DESIGNS TRILOGY

DANGEROUS DESIGNS
Beverly Dale Mayer
Valley Publishing Ltd.
Copyright © 2011

ISBN: 978-1-988315-97-3
Print Edition

About This Book

Drawing is her world…but when her new pencil comes alive, it's his world too.

Her… Storey Dalton is seventeen and now boyfriendless after being dumped via Facebook. Drawing is her escape. It's like as soon as she gets down one image, a dozen more are pressing in on her. Then she realizes her pictures are almost drawing themselves…or is it that her new pencil is alive?

Him… Eric Jordan is a new Ranger and the only son of the Councilman to his world. He's crossed the veil between dimensions to retrieve a lost stylus. But Storey is already experimenting with her new pencil and what her drawings can do – like open portals.

It… The stylus is a soul-bound intelligence from Eric's dimension on Earth and uses Storey's unsuspecting mind to seek its way home, giving her an unbelievable power. She unwittingly opens a third dimension, one that held a dangerous predatory species banished from Eric's world centuries ago, releasing these animals into both dimensions.

Them… Once in Eric's homeland, Storey is blamed for the calamity sentenced to death. When she escapes, Eric is ordered to bring her back or face that same death penalty. With nothing to lose, can they work together across dimensions to save both their worlds?

Sign up to be notified of all Dale's releases here!
https://geni.us/DaleNews

Dedication

This book is dedicated to my daughter Kara, who asked me to write books for her. Dangerous Designs is the third young adult series I have started for her.

Enjoy!

Acknowledgments

Dangerous Designs wouldn't have been possible without the support of my friends and family. Many hands helped with proofreading, editing, and beta reading to make this book come together. I had a vision, but it took many people to make that vision real.

I thank you all

CHAPTER 1

SOME DAYS JUST sucked. Then there was today – with a whole new level of bad. Storey Dalton, sixteen, was now boyfriendless.

Jeff had moved away from Bankhead six months ago, but in her mind, they were still a couple – until his Facebook message this morning. Like what was she supposed to do with that? He had a new girlfriend and wanted her to be happy for him. She stomped a hapless weed in front of her. The girl's name was Pam. Who called their kid Pam? Sounded like her mother's cooking spray.

The sun shone down so brightly its reflection off the creek blinded her. And of course she'd forgotten her sunglasses. Swearing, she headed to the shady side of the path through the woods where the poplars grew tall and straight. Halfway to school meant halfway to nowhere today.

Jeff had been her best friend first, and then finally her boyfriend. But only for the last couple of months. They'd no sooner made that magical development in their relationship when she found out his family was moving. So what if they were apart? Wasn't true love supposed to survive everything? Even she couldn't hold back a snicker at that thought. *True love my ass.* The only truth here was that Jeff was no longer hers. She could spit she was so mad.

She kicked at a rock in her way, then kicked it again

when her first attempt failed to make it move. Just like her life. The town of Bankhead was dying. The mine had closed, and everyone cute or interesting had moved away. The place was a ghost town. There were less than a couple of hundred kids in school now. And that covered all twelve grades.

Her prospects weren't looking too bright at finding a replacement boyfriend. Tall and slim to the point of being almost skinny, she wasn't exactly a raving beauty – all elbows and knees. Jeff had called her unique, an artist with an interesting perspective on life.

She pulled her leg back and lashed out at a bigger rock – hard. *Damn, that felt good.* Grinning, she went a little wild and kicked the shit out of a good half dozen stones. Reveling in the solid slap against her foot and the hefty force she could apply, Storey struck out at life, her lack of friends, and most of all at her current boyfriendless state.

The last kick did it. A pressure gauge in her chest released and she laughed as the weight slid off her shoulders. "He's found someone else, fine. So will I. So it may not be today or tomorrow, but I'll find someone too."

As she passed another big rock she seriously thought about giving it a good whack, when a glint beside it caught her eye.

A pencil. She grinned in delight. She loved pencils. Had a shoebox full in her bedroom. Picking it up, she brushed some loose dirt off. Unusually flat with a well-loved look to it, the bare nub of lead showing spoke to the artist in her. "Cool. We're a well-matched pair. Both tossed away by those we love." With a sense of kinship, she zipped it safely into the side pocket of her backpack and headed off to school.

THREE DAYS LATER Storey had had it with Bankhead High School, her supposed friends, and especially her teachers. They weren't horrible. They were worse – at least today when any and all distractions were unacceptable.

Couldn't they see she was busy?

Her artwork demanded her attention.

"Storey, please stay after school so we can talk, again," said Mr. Madison, the history teacher.

A twitter rippled through the room. Storey ignored him, flicking a look of disgust to the room in general; she refocused on the design she had to get down. She called them doodles. Other people called them freaky. Not that she cared. She'd been drawing since she could hold a pencil. She wasn't about to stop now.

She couldn't. In a small corner of her mind, she knew that wasn't normal. That same corner of her mind knew this drive, this insane need to draw above all else was seriously wrong.

But it didn't matter.

With a toss of her shoulder-length hair, she bent her head to deepen the inside edge of a curlicue.

She heard the teacher's heavy, long suffering sigh. "All right, everyone. Read over the next chapter and do the first ten questions for practice. We'll go over the answers tomorrow. Class dismissed. Except for Storey."

Damn. She glanced up quickly, caught the smirks of the kids walking by. She needed just a few more moments. The pencil warmed in her hand. She quickly readjusted her grip and sketched faster. The amused looks in her direction didn't deserve acknowledgement.

The room emptied in a crush of movement and excited chatter until only silence filled the room – and the scratch of her pencil.

Mr. Madison strode down the aisle of desks until he stood before her. His hands burrowed deep in his pockets as he rocked on his heels. "Storey," he snapped. "Put down that pencil and talk to me."

Disgusted, Storey tossed the pencil down and slouched back so she could see him. Tall, almost droopy, his normally placid face had pulled in on itself as if a lemon had been shoved inside. Wrinkles furrowed his brow as he glowered down at her behind his seriously thick glasses.

"You've been in my class for six weeks. You hand in all your assignments and you did well on your test. You're often distracted, but these last few days…I just don't get it. It's like you're off in your own little world." Frustration twisted his face tighter. Storey watched in fascination as the skin folds expanded then folded back up as he spoke again. "Why can't you pay attention?"

This again. She shook her head. "I can't. That's why I draw." Irritation took over. "I've already told you that. I have trouble focusing." Closing her book with a snap, she stood up only then seeing she'd already picked the pencil up again and was doodling on her fingers. Weird. The pencil marks shouldn't show up on her skin. She glanced up at her teacher. "It's not just your class. It's all my classes."

His shoulders slumped and some of the anger drained from his voice. "Have you spoken to a doctor about this?"

"I've been on every kind of drug there is since first grade. Nothing has worked. Now I don't take anything. What's the point? I have two years to go, then it won't be a problem anymore." She bent down, grabbed her backpack and put away her sketchbook and homework. Straightening, she stood up and waited to see if he had anything to add.

"You have a future. You're smart, a hard worker, at least in the short term, but don't you want to do more – be more?"

His words haunted her long after she'd walked out of the building.

"Of course, I want more, damn it. Who doesn't?" she said to the empty sidewalk. But who could think about the future when the present was such a mess? Sure, she had her mother, somewhat. She had no siblings, for which she was both sad and grateful at the same time. They would have been company, except then they'd be in her same situation, and she wouldn't wish that on anyone. Who'd want to be the kid of the poor single mom despised by the rest of the community? It's not that she thought there was anything wrong with her mother's choices, but being a practicing Wiccan and owning and running a small candle shop in a redneck town like this one, well…not fun.

She kinda liked the emptiness of the skeleton community left at Bankhead. Except for the limited options in friends and boyfriends, of course. The traffic was calm, there were no lines at any of the stores, and nothing bad ever happened. Of course, nothing good ever happened, either.

She picked up her pace and managed to cut her trip home by half. Her latest doodle had its claws into her. True, that was an odd way to describe this gnawing inside to draw, but it felt right. After finishing a picture, she usually experienced an incredible sense of satisfaction and release. That part felt good, the actual creation part – not so much. These last few days, there'd been no satisfaction. In fact, the process had been so much worse. Past driven. Tormented might be a better term.

Her mother believed she'd outgrow her weird doodles

and become a real artist eventually. A large rock went flying into the creek at her side as she contemplated that concept. How did you outgrow something that was a major part of yourself? It's not like she could outgrow a leg, or her hands. They were just as much an integral part of who she was as this compulsion to draw. An urge that had gotten much worse lately. A fact that was starting to make her seriously uneasy. Being an artist was fine with her, being obsessive about it – not so much.

"Hey, Storey?"

Storey spun around but continued to walk backwards. A tall man in black was walking up behind her. She frowned and reassessed her first impression. Not a man, a teen on the brink of adulthood. And one oddly familiar. Right. He was the new kid at school, a rare enough event that it caught even her attention. She'd caught a glimpse of him in the morning, navigating through the hallways. Tall and slim, dressed in black from top to toe, even his short hair matched, giving his white skin a bleached look in contrast. He'd make a perfect vampire.

She couldn't help but smile. "Hi." For the life of her she couldn't remember his name. Her eyes locked on his square jaw, deep forehead and blazing blue eyes. His face would be hard to forget.

A lopsided grin slipped out, fascinating her.

"I'm Eric. You probably don't remember me. I just started at school today." He fell into step as she continued on her way.

"This is your first day and you know *my* name."

"I recognized a fellow artist in the first class we shared and…" His smile deepened. "Your name would be hard *not* to know after the number of times I heard a teacher call it out today."

"Oh." Heat crawled up her face. Her stride stretched out, making him increase his pace to keep up.

"Sorry. Didn't mean to upset you."

Surprised, she shot him a quick sideways glance. "You didn't. Everyone knows I spend most of my time caught up in my art. Getting yelled at is no big deal."

The same grin flowed in her direction. She watched, captivated at how his face changed with his moods. Her fingers itched for pencil and paper. His voice was striking too, gravelly with a sense of humor lurking just beneath the surface.

"What? Am I wearing my lunch on my face or something?" He swiped his chin self-consciously.

Her eyes widened. "Sorry. I didn't mean to stare," she muttered and walked even faster.

"Hey slow down, we're not racing anywhere. And you're tall, but I'm taller."

Confused, she slowed down, sliding a sideways glance his way. "What does height have to do with it?"

"That I can walk as fast as you, I just don't want to."

Yeah, he was weird. "You don't have to walk with me at all." She couldn't help but point that out. Give him a chance to beg off and go his own way. It was kind of hard to believe he was still there in the first place.

"I know. I want to."

She snorted. "And why would you want to do that?"

"Because I like your artwork. It's unique, dark."

This time there was no holding back the look of disbelief. "And you like dark art?"

"Yup. It's cool." They came to a corner. "This is where I turn off. I live just down there." In spite of herself, Storey looked in the direction he pointed. He lived close to the old mine. Not the most affluent area of town. Still, it wasn't loser city like where she lived.

"See you tomorrow." He waved and walked away.

Storey crossed the road, watching as his lanky frame disappeared in the distance.

What was that all about?

A horn blasted her. She jumped and spun around. Crap. She'd stopped in the middle of the intersection like a lovestruck idiot. With an apologetic smile, she moved out of the way and finished the trip home in irate confusion. What the hell was going on with her these days?

Once inside, she stormed up to her room. Flinging her backpack onto her bed, she pulled out her sketchbook and her new pencil and threw herself down on her purple coverlet to stare at her latest drawing.

Cool. Dark. Unique. His words. There was nothing cool about it. Terrifying. Crazy. Disturbing. Any and all of those worked and so much more besides. She stuffed her newest pencil behind her ear and tried to see something that was good in the picture. Coiling, snake-like lines and lattice intertwined, showing an entrance of some kind, broken and abused, as if someone had pounded on it for a long time – and had given up.

Tucking the pencil into her fingers, she started shading the broken slat on the top corner. It didn't look quite right, yet. But how could she know? She'd never seen this place before.

Her subconscious spawned this stuff. Was she crazy? She felt like it most of the time. Lord knows, everyone else agreed. Except her mom. And Jeff had never appeared to notice. At least he'd never said anything about it to her.

Since he'd moved, she'd buried herself deeper into her sketches to help deal with the pain of his leaving and the loneliness she'd been left with. Only in these last few days had she'd realized just how deep she'd gone.

Her pencil shifted to shade the edges of the lattice on the right. Thickening it, darkening it, smoothing the top piece and dropping the bottom down lower. Time ceased to exist as she fine-lined and perfected the image.

"Storey? Are you in there?"

Storey reared back with a jerk, looking around to see her mother poke her head around the door.

"Hi, honey." Her mom pushed the door back and walked in, her long, metallic-orange dress swirling around her legs, her brown hair bouncing off her hips. "What are you doing?"

Draw. Storey. Draw.

"Nothing," her standard response to her mom's standard question.

"Oh, that's a nice picture."

Storey raised an eyebrow. Nice? That's the last thing it was. Typical of her mom though. "No Mom, it's not nice. It's not anything."

"Oh, honey. Don't be so hard on yourself. You'll work your way through all this. Soon you'll draw nice pictures."

Come, finish it. Draw, Storey, draw.

Storey closed her eyes and let her mother drone on. She would no matter what. Finally, she interrupted the flow by asking, "Did you want something?"

Her mom stopped, her mouth open, and cleared her throat. "Oh, yes – dinner's ready."

Opening her eyes again, Storey wrinkled up her face. "I'm not hungry."

"That's not fair." Her mother's voice changed, cajoled. "You don't even know what's for dinner."

"It doesn't matter." Storey rolled over to her belly and continued with her drawing. Her mother gave one of those heavy sighs she was so good at before withdrawing.

Come play with me, Storey.

Storey glared down at the artwork. "I'm here. I'm here. What do you want from me?"

Draw. Just draw.

Storey fell back under the creative spell.

CHAPTER 2

URING SCHOOL THE next day, Storey struggled against exhaustion. She'd slept badly, having awakened over a dozen times. Her eyelids drooped. The teacher spoke, startling her awake. She straightened, blinking several times, her gaze instinctively dropping to her backpack on the floor and the sketchbook tucked inside. With a slight shudder, she returned her attention to the blackboard and the lesson of the day. She could survive this class. It shouldn't be that hard. She dropped her head backwards and groaned. The next two years stretched before her in dismal eternity.

"What are you drawing?"

Surprised, she twisted around to find Eric grinning at her from the seat behind hers.

"You're awake, I see."

She flushed and faced the front of the class. He wouldn't stop.

"I asked what you're drawing?"

"I'm not drawing anything," she muttered.

"Then what's that?" He nudged her right shoulder and pointed to the open page of the red binder in front of her.

Straightening in shock, she realized every inch of space on the paper crawled with pencil lines. She'd deliberately kept her sketchbook stuffed deep inside her backpack and still she'd found a way to keep at it – by filling up her notebook.

Ice settled in her belly.

Did this drive…this need to draw have such a strong hold on her that she couldn't *not* draw? That she did it when not realizing? Even on her skin, like on her fingers yesterday when there'd been no paper near? Was she that obsessed? If so, how had it happened? When? Had there been a specific point of no return?

"I like it. What is it?"

She had no idea. Storey studied the familiar looking scribbles. The markings had the same style, yet in no way resembled the full page drawing she'd done last night. Or did they? Frowning, she realized this picture could represent an enlargement of one corner of that other picture, incorporating her geography class notes into the design. She slammed her book shut.

"Hey? Why'd you do that?"

The teacher ended class at that moment. Storey jumped to her feet, snagging her backpack in one hand and notebook in the other before racing out of the room.

"Wait up!"

Eric's voice became lost in the crowd. Good. She hadn't planned on listening to it anyway.

THIS WAS AN easy job?

A simple job, Paxton had said to him and his father. "Go find the girl. Become friends with her, and if she has the stylus – retrieve it. Preferably, without her knowing. You're close to her age, so it should be easy to gain her confidence. The important thing is to bring the stylus home. Before the girl causes irreparable harm through her ignorance."

Eric Jordan had jumped at the opportunity, not giving his father, the Councilman, a chance to argue. Not that he would have. Eric had studied all he could, become the best Ranger he could be. Even more, he'd become an expert on the alternate dimension. Yet in all that time, he'd never been allowed to cross the veil that separated the two worlds. This was a great first assignment. How hard could it be?

Harder than he'd thought. Storey was turning out to be an interesting female. He'd been watching her for a couple of days now. He got along well with girls. They considered him friendly, caring, comfortable to talk to. What wasn't there to like? But if that were all true, why was this one so prickly? Then again, she was an otherworlder. That could account for the difference.

And he suspected she *did* have the lost instrument, making his mentor Paxton's guess correct. If her drawings were anything to go by, the stylus had started bonding already. Not good. The tool had been lost when a scientist had fallen ill on a rare research trip across the veil that divided the two dimensions. Soulbound items were special in his world. Important, coveted, and passed from one person to another only through death. They were also incredibly powerful. Not something to be left in the hands of a sixteen-year-old otherworld girl.

He watched as Storey bolted from the classroom as if demons were chasing her. Had that been fear tightening her fine-boned features as she'd studied at her artwork?

Why? She'd created it.

Or had she?

STOREY RAN STRAIGHT home. She burst through the front

door and came to a skittering stop. Her mother's Wiccan friends were meeting in the living room. Great. On the other hand, their presence gave her an excuse to hide away in her room and sort through these odd drawings. See if there was a connection in them. A message.

And that was just stupid.

"Storey. How nice to see you home early." Her mother, decked out in her ceremonial robes and her face covered in heavy paint, walked over. "Why don't you join us, sweetie?" She motioned toward her friends, all in full Wiccan gear. "We're going over the weekend's events."

It was all Storey could do not to wince. Giving the others a quick smile, she brushed past her mom. "No time. I have homework."

She raced up the stairs and into her room, slamming the door behind her. No wonder everyone thought she was odd. Look at her mother. She'd been shunned and taunted when younger. Now most of the other kids just crossed the road to avoid her. Then there were the whispers and sidelong looks. Odd how her relationship with Jeff had brought acceptance. Until he'd left.

Life had been normal until her father had walked out a decade ago, leaving her homemaker mom struggling to make a living. Her mother had been 'finding herself' ever since. The store and a new religion had been her answer. As much as Storey hated what it had done to her life, she understood that the candle shop had put food on the table all these years. The Wiccan part, not so much. Her mother held some rank on the Council and, of course, she dressed the part, even danced outside on full moons. Storey did not want to know if the group did it naked.

Some things were just too much information.

She pulled her sketchbook out of her backpack, then grabbed her red binder from class. She plunked down on her bed and flipped through the pages in both books. And stopped. Yes.

Leaning close, she studied the images. The newer one *was* an enlargement of the lower right hand corner of the bigger drawing, where she'd run out of paper. Odd how ancient the doorway in her pictures looked. She rarely drew anything medieval or historical looking and had no idea why she would have now. What did it mean?

Tracing the picture with her fingertips, she tried to understand why it was so important to sketch such detail. Her fingers moved slower and slower in a repetitive and oddly mesmerizing motion. She lost herself in the movement, feeling soothed and comforted by the knowledge that, if nothing else, she'd created this.

A tapping on the window drew her attention. The sun had gone behind a cloud. Even as she watched, rain pelted the glass, giving everything an oddly distorted look. Kind of matched her life right now. With a sigh she refocused on the large sketch.

She stopped. Then frowned. Had the picture changed? Shifted? Bending her head, she studied it closer, then shook her head. No. It was the same. At least she thought so. Anything else was so not possible. As she went to close her books, she paused again.

There. A new line. She studied the picture. She hadn't drawn it – or had she? Stupid, that's what this was. If she hadn't, who had? She had to have put it there. Tilting her head to look at it from another angle, she realized the line still wasn't quite right. She snatched up her pencil and thickened the left side of it, widening it on the bottom.

There, that was much better. It felt right.

Silly maybe, but the change made her happy.

She switched to staring at the weird enlarged picture she'd made in class today. With the geography notes underneath, it was irritating to look at. Within minutes, she had redrawn the picture into her sketchbook properly. Now that she could see it more clearly, she realized it *was* an actual door of some kind. Not just a vague entranceway. Now it had defined edges. Without a latch or knob, yet the right size and shape. She laughed at her imagination. So there was a door. Now wouldn't it be great if that meant she could just open the door and walk right through?

The last thing she did was add a flat, metal looking door handle to the right side.

Snick.

Storey glanced at her bedroom door. "Mom, is that you?" Her door was closed and stayed that way. More unnerved by her reaction than at the noise, Storey hopped up and checked to see if someone stood outside her room.

The hallway was empty. Laminate floors and red and gold painted walls stared back at her, remnants of the previous owners.

Closing her door on the horrible colors, Storey surveyed her own lemon and lavender room. So much easier on her eyes. The rain continued to hit the window, filling the room with a steady pounding. With everything as it should be, she sat back down on the bed and picked up her drawing.

And caught her breath. She'd put the handle in as a joke.

It was no joke now. The freaking door was open. She peered closer. At least she thought it was open. The edge of the door was now a thick black line hinting at a darkness on the other side.

She dropped the book on her bed and bolted to the far side of the room. She chewed her nails, not taking her eyes off her picture. The open door stared back at her.

An open door she hadn't drawn. She knew that. Still, she couldn't stop a quick glance at the pencil in her hand. Just in case. There was no way. Really? How could those couple of lines give off such an ominous vibe? With so much power? Chills rippled across her shoulders.

Inviting her? Warning her? Freaking her out – *hell yeah!*

Storey knew she wasn't that good an artist.

Could she be having blackouts? Momentary relief bloomed at the idea. Then she reached up and touched her temple. She didn't suffer from headaches. She hadn't been injured. As far as she knew, she was healthy.

How could the picture have changed without her or someone else changing it? And why? She studied the lines of the door. Flat, thick lined, almost needing something from her. Waiting for her to do something. But what?

It's not like she could walk through the thing. And even if she could, it's not like she would. Who knew what lay on the other side? A half chuckle escaped. Right. Now she *was* losing it.

Storey grimaced as she shoved the drawing deep inside her bag, then closed and tied up the outside straps as a deterrent. Determined, she grabbed her English reading assignment and focused on finishing her homework. When she couldn't keep her eyes open any longer, she dropped the book to the floor beside her, clicked off the light and fell into a deep sleep – a sleep full of weird dreams and strange voices calling to her.

Storey, come and get me.

Storey come.

We need you, Storey.

Disturbed, she bolted upright, gasping for breath. She stared wildly around the room. Who said that? No one. She was alone – and clearly losing it. Her heart banged in her chest. A film of sweat covered her skin. She took several deep breaths and tried to calm down. Talk about nightmares. She shuddered and lay back down. It took several minutes to get her breathing under control and when she did, she started to get pissed.

"What the hell do you want with me?" she snapped in the direction of her backpack and the drawing safely secured inside. "Crap. This is too freaky, even for me."

"Storey, is that you, honey?"

Her mother knocked on the door and pushed it open, the light from the hallway lighting the few silver strands in her otherwise brown hair. "Can't you sleep?"

"Sorry if I woke you." Storey sat up, brushing her own jet black hair back off her face. "Just a bad dream."

"That's because you didn't have any dinner. I checked up on you after the meeting finished. You'd fallen asleep." Her mother's fingers twisted around a dangling lock of hair as she stepped into the room. She bit her lip. "Storey, you have to eat. You're already skinny enough."

Bone rack is what a jock had called her last month. Looking down, Storey realized they could be right. Her hip bones stuck out to match her big elbows. And her body had developed to the point where she barely missed the skinny scarecrow look. Too bad. She might have been able to make that work.

"I'm eating, Mom. They had pizza in class today, so I didn't need my lunch. Ate that on the way home." That was a lie. Still, she had more important things to worry about than food.

Relief washed over her mom's pretty face. "Oh, I'm so glad to hear that. Sometimes I worry about you."

Sometimes? Didn't she mean all the time? Was that normal for moms? Then again, there was a world of difference between normal and her mother.

"What time is it?" Storey looked out the window. Blackness stared back.

"It's just a little after midnight. Please get into your pajamas. You don't want to be sleeping in those jeans." She backed up to the open door. "If you're all right, I'll say good night. It is witching hour, after all." With a carefree grin, her mom closed the door.

Witching hour. Right. Only in her house. Sighing at her mother's antics, Storey collapsed down on her covers and fell into a light, troubled sleep.

"Storey."

She sighed. "What now, Mom?"

No answer. She sat up and glanced at the closed door. Weird. She could've sworn she'd heard someone calling her. Lying down again, she pulled her blankets over top, not bothering to get changed into her nightclothes.

"Storey."

She bolted upright. *That's it.* Who the hell was playing games with her?

"Storey."

Throwing back the blankets, Storey knelt on her bed. "Who said that?" she hissed into the early morning air. Not trusting the gloomy light, she flicked her bedside lamp on, quickly scanning the room. Empty. "I am so losing it. This is nuts."

Her gaze landed on the backpack on her floor. Her eyes

widened. *Oh no.*

"No, no. Hell, no." She shook her head, slowly at first then more wildly. "This can't be happening. It's a picture. Nothing more. Nothing less. I created you. I can destroy you."

That's exactly what she was going to do. She dragged the backpack onto her bed and opened it. The knot defied her first and second attempts, before she managed to pull the laces apart and yank out her sketchpad. "I don't know what's going on here, but enough is enough."

She flipped to the last page she'd been working on and grabbed it at the top left and pulled. It wouldn't tear off. She tightened her grip and tried again. It refused to budge. Scared now, she threw it on the floor and in a fit of defiance, she jumped on it.

And fell through the picture, through the floor even.

She went right through the doorway in her picture.

Chapter 3

A ND LANDED IN complete nothingness.

Storey's knees buckled. She pitched forward, barely catching her balance, and froze. What just happened? Suffocating blackness surrounded her. No bed, no lamp, no floor even. No glimpse of the moon or the rising sun peeked through in any direction. Looking up, she searched for the broken planks of her floor or ceiling tiles from the basement. Something to prove she'd fallen through the bedroom floor.

There was nothing.

"Hello?" Silence. The first stirrings of panic slipped down her spine. Taking a deep breath, she struggled to stay calm, to understand. There was no easing of the unrelenting darkness in any direction. Somehow, she'd ended up in a pitch black, empty hole.

Her bedroom had disappeared. And this space had appeared. Her stomach threatened to spill its contents, bile climbing her throat. Her imagination couldn't help jumping from one wild scenario to the next, each worse than the one before. From thinking she'd fallen through the basement, to the idea of being caught between the floors – like, could you go in-between? She even considered that she might have tripped and fallen into a hidden store room.

She wasn't even going to consider that she might have been abducted by aliens.

This couldn't be happening.

Yet it had.

She swallowed. Then swallowed again. Closing her eyes for a moment, she struggled to remember what she'd done. The last thing she remembered was throwing that damned picture on the floor and jumping on it. On it? On the opening? Therefore on the doorway. And through it?

Her eyelids popped open.

Could she have jumped through a picture of a door as if it were a real exit? She shook her head as her mind stretched and reached the impossible conclusion.

And if she had…where was she now? Where did that strange passageway lead?

Wherever the hell she was, she'd damned well better find a way out. Once she realized her eyes couldn't adjust to the all-encompassing darkness, she reached out, her arms wide, hoping to find something solid. Her fingers twitched as her mind filled with thoughts of the many unpleasant things she could encounter. Spiders being the number one yucky critter in her world.

Nothing. She'd entered a space where she alone existed. Panic brought the acid in her stomach bubbling back up. This had to be a dream. A nightmare. She brightened. Maybe when she jumped on the sketchbook, she'd fallen and hit her head. Maybe she had a concussion? That had to be it. Eagerly she checked her head for blood, at minimum some tenderness.

Her skull was as thick-headed as she was. Storey groaned. "Please, someone," she cried out. "Is anyone out there?"

Eerie echoes went on forever.

She shuddered, the blackness threatening to suffocate

her. She bent over and breathed once, twice, three times until the rapids in her stomach calmed down. As she stared down where her feet should be, it hit her. The floor was solid. Stomping to prove it, she crouched down to touch the surface. Hard, cold wood or maybe even tile supported her. It gave her hope.

Someone had built it. That meant people. Somewhere.

She had to have fallen into a storage space or something, a closet even. Okay, that would mean one huge-ass closet, but it was possible. She took one deliberate step. She stretched her arms forward. Still nothing. Bending down, she touched the ground and crabbed forward, her hands making sure there was something for her to stand on before taking the next step.

She continued for another ten steps. And stood up.

Was the darkness less cloying? She sniffed the air. Still bad, musty. She put out her hands again – still nothing. Fisting her hands on her hips, she stood and contemplated the situation. *What a piss off.* Where the hell was she? And as much as she'd like to understand how she'd gotten here, the priority was getting out.

And fast.

"WHAT IS SHE doing?" Eric tilted his head to study Storey's sideways crab imitation on the monitor in front of him, a frown crinkling his forehead. He'd rushed into the lab at Paxton's panicked call, only to come to a halt in front of the wall sized screen that showed Storey inside a crossing.

"I have no idea," Paxton retorted. "She wouldn't be doing even that, if you'd kept an eye on her."

"Hey," Eric protested. "That's not fair. You didn't even

think she could *do* something like this. How was I to know?"

An irritated "Harrumph," from beside him was his only answer.

"So now what?"

"We watch."

Shooting a sideways glance at Paxton, Eric struggled not to scrunch up his face in disgust. "Uhm, isn't that a little mean?"

Paxton beetled his brows. "Mean? How are we going to know what she can do if we don't watch her and find out?"

"I don't think she has any idea of what she can do. Look at her. She's afraid she's going to run out of floor and fall off."

"And she might. If she'd created that."

The younger man gave him an incredulous look. "You can't possibly think she did this on purpose?"

"Right." Paxton shook his head in his far too familiar *I taught you better than that* way.

"Honest. I've spent days watching her. She's a good artist, yes, but she creates mindlessly"

"Then how did she create a portal?"

Eric paused and chose his next words carefully. "I think it's the stylus."

"What are you talking about?"

"I think it's bonding with her."

Complete shock rendered the old man silent. "Oh my. How is that possible? Do you know for sure that she has it? You've actually seen it in her hand?" He spun around to study Storey's movements in the tunnel. "It *can't* become soulbound to her. She's not one of us."

"I think I saw it. She wouldn't let me take a close look. This," Eric waved at the monitor, "proves it. It's the only way she could open a portal."

The older man shuddered. "This is not good."

"I'm assuming the stylus is trying to come home?"

At his mentor's gasping cough, Eric turned to stare at the red splotches appearing on Paxton's face. "Are you okay?"

"No. No, I'm not," he snapped. "This is terrible. Something has to be done. She can't come here. She's one of *them*." He almost spat the last word.

And? Eric didn't see that they had a choice. The stylus had latched onto Storey and appeared to be coming home whether Paxton approved or not. In fact, according to the monitor, the two of them had almost made it.

Eric watched as Storey bent once more to the floor and crabbed her way forward. "We have to do something. This is painful to watch."

The older man pivoted. "This can't happen. That the stylus was lost in the first place is unacceptable. That one of those otherworlders should have picked it up is worse…that the stylus is accepting…even strengthening the bond is…" Paxton stopped talking, overcome by emotion. He pressed his trembling fingers against his temples.

"It might change things if we assist her, you know." Eric gestured at Storey. "Chances are, she'd appreciate the help."

A calculating look brightened Paxton's slate blue eyes. He rubbed his hands together. "Yes. Yes, that might work. She already knows you. You could cross over and let her out on *her* side of the veil."

Eric considered the logistics. "She hasn't exactly welcomed me so far. A rescue could do a lot to help that."

Paxton nodded. "She can't be allowed to find out the power of the stylus. Get it away from her."

"It might already be too late. If she's soulbound already, we can't separate them. You know that," he countered.

The old man wrung his hands as he considered the problem. "Certainly we can. We have to. The stylus is too powerful. Too dangerous. But first things first. Get her out of the crossing and retrieve the stylus."

Eric shook his head. "I'm not going to participate in anything that will cause her death."

Paxton straightened to his full height and stared down his long nose at Eric. "Then go. The longer the two are together, the harder it will be to separate them. Get the stylus now and she lives. Don't get it and she dies. Either way that stylus has to come home."

With that order, Eric adjusted his soulkey, tapped into his codex and shifted dimensions.

STOREY WAS BEYOND pissed and had jumped completely into terror. Something had gone majorly wrong in her world. And she didn't know how to reverse it. Initially anger had held the fear in check, but now it clogged her throat and clouded her vision. She'd gone from being warm and cozy on top of her bed to lost in this dark hole, a chill settling into her bones. The thought of being stuck in this blackness forever kept shudders creeping up and down her spine. Please, let this not be the end of her world.

The world had to be out there somewhere. No direction appeared to be a better bet than any other. She couldn't just stand still forever.

"Hello? Is someone there?"

Storey spun around, excited relief blasting through her. "Help! Hello? Can someone hear me?"

"Hang on. I'm coming."

Oh thank God. She was saved! Storey couldn't believe it. Someone must have heard her screams. She glanced down at her jeans, relieved that she wasn't in her usual sleepwear – a camisole and matching shorts. To think she'd almost changed for bed. Then again, she might not have been found at all.

The darkness in front of her lightened. Storey pivoted to see a slice of sunlight opening up behind her. The strip widened, highlighting the old worn plank floor at her feet. Weird. She dashed to the doorway, open enough just enough for her to slip through, and blinked in the bright light. The sun crested the familiar shape of her mountain top. It was morning? How long had she been in there?

She turned to look at her rescuer.

Eric.

His grin flashed, that killer look of pure bad boy. Like he'd just come off a hot night. She gulped. The goose bumps on her arms had to be from the cool mountain air.

"Hey, Storey. What the hell were you doing in there?"

"In where?"

Storey spun around and studied the door she'd just exited. It didn't look like the one in her picture. In fact, it looked like an ordinary plain old door. Wood, some kind of cut molding running around the edge and a standard issue round door knob. The door attached to a large front wall of some kind. No sign identified the purpose or location. Stripped of paint and worn, the whole thing had an abandoned look to it.

"Where am I?" Puzzled, she backed up to get a wider view of the building. "What is this place?"

"It's an abandoned mine entrance."

She spun around. "It's what?"

Eric pointed out the landmarks. "This is the trailer entrance to the old Bankhead mine. Remember, it closed down a few years back?"

"How do you know? I thought you were new?" she murmured with a sidelong glance. Way off topic, but the fact that she could actually keep a conversation going right now was a freakin' miracle. So what if it was a mine entrance? What she really wanted to know was how the hell she'd managed to get inside.

"If you didn't know what the place was, how did you get inside?"

Trying for an air of nonchalance she didn't feel, Storey went for simplicity. "I fell down a hole, ended up in the mine."

A long slow whistle escaped his lips, his eyes widened in shock. "Wow. Good thing I found you when I did. You could have been stuck in there forever."

Oh, God. He was right. A shudder worked up her legs, reducing them to the consistency of wet noodles. But as much as she wanted to bolt from the place, she knew she had to have answers. Otherwise, what would stop her from ending up there again? She needed to go back in – with the door open for light.

"Come on, let's go home." Eric faced the wide, gravel road overgrown by bushes and weeds.

Storey glanced from the door to the road then back to the door. She had to know. "Just a second."

A few quick steps and she had her hand on the doorknob before she could talk herself out of it. It wouldn't open. She frowned and spun back to Eric. "Did you lock it again?"

"Lock what?" He walked back and tested the door himself. It wouldn't open. "No. I didn't. At least, I don't think so."

"Freaky," she murmured. The door *was* old and rusty. Eric stood off to one side, hands on his hips, glaring at her. Had he locked it to stop her from going back inside? Then why not just say so? Or maybe he'd locked it accidentally.

"Are you coming?"

"Yeah," she said with one long last look at the door.

She'd explore later. When Eric wasn't around. And when she had a flashlight.

Something beyond weird was going on and she needed to know what it was.

CHAPTER 4

SCHOOL SLOGGED BY. Storey was desperate to get home, yet every time she checked her watch, it appeared to have stopped, forcing her to check the clock on the back wall.

"Yes, Storey, it's at least two minutes since you last checked the time. What's the matter? Do you have a hot date or something?"

Snickers raced around the classroom, gaining momentum until they became an outright laugh.

"She's probably heading to the coven for her initiation." That comment came from somewhere off to the left. Storey didn't bother looking for the culprit. Could be any one of a dozen people hitting at her because of her mother.

Laughter swelled.

Stone-faced, she slouched lower in her seat. To hell with them.

"So if we have everyone's attention again," Mr. Morrison continued with a smirk, "there's going to be a quiz on chapters eleven and twelve tomorrow. Study and do well. Don't study, don't care and maybe fail. Everyone is dismissed." He waved good-bye before wiping off the blackboard.

Letting the class empty ahead of her, Storey took her time to collect her stuff. The last thing she wanted was to attract any more attention.

"Nice pencil. Can I see it?" Eric's long, black, jean-clad legs showed up beside her desk as she crouched to repack her overstuffed backpack.

Storey snatched the pencil off her seat where she'd set it and slipped it into the side pocket of her bag before zipping it shut. "It's a pencil. Nothing special."

Eric studied her face. "An art pencil?"

"Nope. Just a pencil."

He raised his left eyebrow. "Then why won't you let me take a look at it?" He waited another moment. "Where did you get it? I'd kinda like one for myself."

"Check the stores. I'm sure someone will carry it." Storey turned and walked out of the classroom.

Paying attention during school had been impossible with memories of her crazy, late-night outing running through her brain. She'd made it home from the mine that morning and raced to her bedroom, only to discover the undamaged sketchbook still lying where she'd thrown it on the floor. She'd stood stunned in her open doorway. No gaping hole in the floor, no damage even.

Of course there wasn't. It couldn't be any other way. Still she couldn't reconcile what had actually happened in her mind. Finding escape in running away, she'd grabbed a change of clothes, a bite to eat and had left for school without waking up her mother. She'd needed time to think. Time to assess what the hell had happened. And why.

All the while, she'd questioned Eric's opportune arrival at the mine entrance. It's not like he'd offered an explanation for his presence there at that hour. Then again, neither had she. Still, as much as she appreciated the rescue, his arrival outside the mine entrance had unlikely coincidence written all over it. She didn't believe in those. Ever.

He was up to something.

Shaking her head, Storey glanced behind her to make sure she was truly alone before racing the last leg home.

Her mother might be a little odd in the eyes of the town folk, but she'd done one thing right – she'd taught Storey common sense. Storey's instincts screamed at her about Eric. He was too good-looking, too interesting and too interested in her to be normal. He was…*different*. Good different or bad different? Too early to tell.

She knew one thing – she wanted to go back into the mine.

Apprehension wafted through her. Okay, so maybe she didn't *want* to go back into the mine. It was more like she *had* to go back in.

Home loomed in front of her. With it came a sense of awe. A sense of joy. A grin split her face. She, Storey Dupont, had a door into a mine shaft through her bedroom floor. She didn't know how and she sure as hell didn't know why, but there it was. And she was going to go through it again – soon.

Well, after a snack and picking up a few supplies.

In the kitchen, she threw back a tall glass of water and opened the cupboard. There were fruit snacks in there somewhere.

"Storey?" Her mom wandered into the room, dressed in lounging pants and a camisole, rubbing sleep from her eyes. Jesus. It was three in the afternoon. Her assistant must be watching the store.

"There you are. Are you all right?"

"Of course, I'm fine, Mom. Why?"

"Well, Gina called this morning and mentioned that she

saw you walking very early this morning with a boy."

Storey glanced over at her mom and caught her deep blue gaze – not accusing Storey, exactly. At least not yet.

"And I know you were in bed last night because we spoke."

Storey turned back to the cupboard without responding. Great. Someone had spotted her and had tattled already. About Eric no less.

After a moment, her mother continued, her voice forced into light casualness. "She was pretty sure she'd recognized you." She cleared her throat. "Did you leave the house early? Without saying anything?" She hesitated. "And with a boy?"

Distracted, Storey struggled to find an answer.

"Storey?"

Storey had to give herself a shake. "Yes, I woke up early and thought I'd go out for a walk. You were asleep when I got back, so I got ready for school and left."

"Oh. Uhm. You're not trying to exercise at that hour, are you?" Her mother moved closer, reaching out a hand to Storey's arm. She peered up into Storey's eyes. "I know you've had a tough couple of months since Jeff moved away, and I know you want to be like the other girls and all, but you're getting so skinny. I'm worried. You're almost anorexic."

"What? No, I'm not. Look, I couldn't sleep so I went down to the creek to watch the sunrise." She reached out and gave her mom a quick hug. "I'm fine. I eat. Honest." Storey hoped the conversation would die a natural death at this point. Her mom had spent most of Storey's preteen years trying to make her 'see the light' in one matter or another.

Storey had always preferred the dark, which might account for her need to get back into that blackness.

She still hadn't figured that trip out. She wanted to try it again, but to enter from the mine side so she could have her exit ready and have the benefit of daylight inside. If Eric had been able to open the door, she should be able to as well. What was the chance of the mine having power and working lights? And then, after checking it out thoroughly from that side, she'd try going through the floor again.

"I have to go out for a bit. What time is dinner? I promise, I'll be home and I'll eat."

"Around six. Where are you going?"

"Just downtown. Maybe buy a new pair of jeans." Like hell. She hated shopping. Still, she had to find some excuse.

"Do you need money?" Her mother brightened at the mention of such a normal, girlie activity. She reached for her purse and pulled out a couple of twenty dollar bills. "Here. I can't think of the last time you asked me for some. You're such a good kid."

Storey knew better than to answer that statement. Pocketing the money, she thanked her mom and headed back outside. She started walking in the direction of the mall. Once out of sight of her home, she changed course and retraced the route she'd taken home with Eric that morning. She knew the area vaguely. When she came to the gravel road, she knew she was on the right track. In her mind, she'd half doubted that the door would even be there. Rounding the bend, she stopped in relief. There it was. She ran the last few yards. At the entrance, she looked around and frowned. This was too accessible. Shouldn't they have made this entrance more secure? To stop kids from going inside.

She tried the door knob. Locked.

No surprise. She opened her backpack and pulled out a thin metal tool she'd gotten from Jeff months ago. They'd watched this cool video that had demonstrated how to pick locks. She'd tried it on her own house and had managed it with both a bobby pin and a credit card. This wire thingy was the best.

Bending down, she studied the side of the knob. This door had a different locking mechanism than the one at home. She frowned. This might not work. She played with the steel pick for several moments, then switched to using her bank card. Still, it wouldn't open. Frustration mounted. She wanted in. Damn it. She studied the surrounding area.

Eric had gotten in. If he could get in, then so could she. Ten minutes later, she had to give it up. The damn thing wouldn't budge.

Hands fisted on her hips, she considered her options. Should she go home and try to enter from her room again? With a flashlight, she should be able to find the door from inside the mine.

This method certainly wasn't getting her anywhere.

The return trip home was fast. She slipped onto the back porch and into the kitchen without letting her mom know. She hurried to her room. Gathering up a piece of chalk and a bottle of water, she searched for her flashlight, finally locating it under the bed. At the last minute, she snatched up her hoodie and checked that she had her cell phone…just in case. Turning her attention to the sketchbook on her floor, she hooked her backpack on her shoulder. Taking a deep breath, Storey hopped onto the bed, stared down at the picture in front of her…and jumped.

She landed on the floor. "Damn it." Scrambling back up onto her bed, she tried again. Nothing. What was wrong? And if it worked once it would work twice. So what was different this time? She considered this issue while standing on her bed, looking down. She'd been scared and angry last time, could that have made the difference? If so, she was getting pretty damned pissed just thinking about it now. She jumped. Nothing. Feeling like an idiot, she climbed up and said, "Open sesame." Then jumped.

Nothing.

Shit.

This was ridiculous. "Why is it not working?" She sat on the edge of her bed, picked up the book and studied the sketch. She bolted upright. "What the hell?"

The door in her sketch was no longer open. Somehow, though her hand hadn't touched a pencil to paper, the door in her drawing now appeared closed.

She hadn't done it herself. Whatever had opened the door – had closed the door. That's why she couldn't get in anymore. The damned door was closed.

Reaching into the backpack, she grabbed up her pencil and tried to make the door in her sketch look open. The pencil wouldn't touch the paper. She flipped to a new page, and tried to copy the sketch onto the fresh paper, only this time with the door open. Except the pencil had a mind of its own and drew the door closed.

Storey sat back.

What was going on here?

Magic?

Satanism?

Surely not. Her mother dabbled in Wiccanism…could she have done something dangerous? Not likely. The religion was all about good not evil – no matter what people thought. The sunlight shone through her bedroom window, brightening the room, making it hard to think on dark and supernatural factors in the face of so much light. She glanced back down at her book. The light shone on the picture, giving it an odd look. Twisting the sketchbook around, she flicked it up and down in the sunbeam. Nothing changed. Her pencil flashed.

She held it up in the weird light. Though it was old and kind of ratty, the kinship she'd felt with it had only strengthened with time. It flashed again. What was that? She bent closer, trying to see what was inscribed on the side. She hadn't even noticed it before. She twisted it slowly in the light. There.

It was some kind of script.

Storey tried to read it. She twisted it around and around. The writing faded when not in the sunlight. In the light, the writing etched itself in as if by some unseen hand.

"So cool," she murmured. "What does it mean?"

And how could she find out? Grabbing a different pencil, she tried to copy the script down on a piece of scrap paper. It took several tries at holding it in the light to get it just right. The inscribed lines didn't appear to be words, per say, or at least not in any language she'd seen before. Numbers? Dates? She didn't know. Taking the scrap of paper downstairs to her mom's computer, she scanned it in, then dragged the image to her flash drive. Back upstairs, she searched the Internet for ancient fonts and languages.

By late afternoon, she'd found nothing. *Damn it.* For the millionth time, she glanced at her floor and wondered if she should try again. She decided against it. The time had disappeared on her and she didn't want to spend the night in that mine. Still…maybe she should. It wasn't *that* late. She hopped off her computer chair and walked closer.

"Storey? Dinner time."

So much for a quick trip into a tunnel, at least for the

moment. "Coming." She put away her stuff and tucked the scrap of paper with the copied script under her keyboard. She couldn't explain why she felt the need to hide it. For the same reason, she'd renamed the scan as Chemistry Paper. That should keep people in the dark. Not that anyone would see it. Still…

She headed downstairs to dinner and dishes. That was another thing that sucked about being an only child – no one to share the chores with.

It took another hour before she could return to her room, telling her mom and her mom's arriving Wiccan friends that she had a lot of homework to do. She rolled her eyes at that lame excuse. When did she ever do homework?

Closing her bedroom door behind her, her gaze caught and held on her sketchbook. Should she try again? The phone rang. Storey ignored it. It was never for her. She had a cell phone like everyone else.

"Storey, answer the phone, please. It's for you."

Storey stilled. Who'd be calling her? On the house phone?

"Storey, did you hear me?"

"Yes. Thanks." She walked to the little stand in the middle of the hallway and picked up the cordless phone, then headed back to her room. "Hello?"

"Storey?"

"Yes." Her frown deepened. She didn't recognize the voice. "Who is this?"

"Eric."

"Eric." She winced. Was that breathy squeaky voice hers? Yikes. "Why are you calling? And why this number?"

He laughed. A deep sound that sent the butterflies in her stomach into flight. *Damn.* That was so not a good thing.

What could he possibly want?

"I wanted to make sure you were all right after being locked in that tunnel. And you didn't give me your cell number."

She flopped on the bed. "What? Oh. Here it is." She rattled off the number of her cell. Although she rarely used it, she'd rather her phone calls were private and off her mother's radar. "And yeah. I'm fine. I wasn't really locked in."

"So what do you call it then? I'd planned on asking you about it today, except you left so quickly, I didn't get a chance."

"Sorry about that. Not to worry, I'm fine," she said lightly. Silence stretched between them. She took a deep breath. She shouldn't say anything. She should keep her mouth shut. "I might go back there."

"What!"

She winced. "You don't have to shriek. God, you sound like a girl."

"Great. Thanks for that." She could almost feel his glare through the phone.

She rolled her eyes and sat up. "There's something weird going on. I want to check it out."

"And get locked in permanently next time?"

"Yeah, now that's one of those weird parts I don't understand. How could you have been passing by at exactly the right moment? Not to mention how could you have opened that door? When I tried, it was locked up tight."

The ensuing silence was ominous. The tone of his voice dropped, giving it a dangerous edge. "You tried to open the door? When?"

"Right after you got me out, remember Then again after

school. I wanted to explore the entrance, only I couldn't open the door. It had a weird lock on it."

"I'd imagine that's to keep people out. Did you ever consider how dangerous it might be to go back to that place?"

"Uhm." She grinned. "Not really."

"Are you always this impulsive?"

She shrugged. "Yeah, maybe."

"I can't believe it. You need a keeper." Outrage shimmered through the phone.

"Like that's going to happen," she scoffed. "And if you don't have any other reason for calling, I'll say good-bye now." She didn't feel like getting chewed out by him any more than she did by one of her teachers.

"Wait. Look, please don't go back into the mine. It's dangerous. I don't want you to get hurt or lost."

Storey lifted an eyebrow and stared down at the phone. He didn't? How'd that happen? "I won't. I'm used to doing things alone."

"I don't care." Exasperation slipped into his voice. "Please don't go alone."

"I have to. There's no one to go with me."

"I will. I'll go with you."

HE HADN'T SAID that, had he? That way? Damn. Yes, he was supposed to get close to her, only he hadn't wanted to get *close* to her. The night sky had deepened, darkened to obsidian. What he really wanted was to protect her from doing something foolish that could impact both their dimensions. But what that could be, he didn't know. Humans had an insatiable curiosity and a self-destructiveness that horrified his people. If they killed themselves off, it wouldn't impact his people. If they killed the planet though, both sides would die.

For that reason, his government had worked hard at not letting Storey's people know they existed. His home had to be protected from the uncontrolled humans. A veil separated their worlds and all access to crossover points had to go through a major vetting process. Only the best of the scientists were allowed over and only with a strict security detail. In this way they could keep watch over the Earth in the human's dimension.

Their shared planet had to be protected. They just didn't know how at this point. The population of his world was less than one percent of Storey's yet still spread across the same area, so hidden surveillance was the only way.

Everything had been in happy harmony for ages, until this. No treachery was involved. Just a simple accident and a scientist had lost something that could put both worlds at risk. A team had been dispatched immediately. They'd followed the inherent energy of the ancient tool to its location only to watch as one of the otherworlders picked it up in front of them.

Storey.

"Eric?"

Eric gave himself a mental shake. He was being an idiot. Storey was his assignment. Any way that made it work, made it right.

"Sorry, I was distracted by something else."

"Yeah, duh."

"I meant it. I'll go with you. We can try to open the door from this side. If that doesn't work, then I don't know what else to try. It worked last time though," he added helpfully.

"Right. I might have another way in. I'm just not sure."

Eric frowned, all his senses on high alert. "How?" His voice sharpened as he realized what she implied. The only other method to enter that tunnel was through a portal.

"There are other entrances. Most old mines have abandoned shafts."

"Hence all those warning signs saying danger. Remember those?"

Her voice deepened, slowed. And she should have. Talk about focus. "You know, I'm not so sure I do."

Great. Now she had selective vision too. "Well, they were there."

"No need to snap at me." She sniffed.

He grinned into the phone. She was starting to grow on him. That defiant streak of hers baffled him. He couldn't help but be intrigued.

"I'm going to try again."

"Try what? The door? Not tonight?" He tried to sound horrified. From what he'd observed, most people on this side of the veil avoided going out in the darkness. His side was the opposite. The sun shone hotly so much of the time that many people preferred to go about in the dark. The geography of both sides was the same, with one sun and one moon, an atmosphere necessary for life and various animals and plant life dotting the countryside. The two peoples resembled each other physically. There the similarities appeared to end.

Storey's people appeared to be less developed. They relied heavily on what they called technology. They appeared to choose their futures by the type of work they liked or the type of work that found them. Giving away their power instead of corralling it and fine-tuning it. He didn't know if they had the same abilities of his kind. Maybe they had died off over the years. In his world, everyone had some special skill, which developed throughout childhood. Once an adult, they were already in their field. They knew what they were meant to do because they'd already been doing it.

He didn't get it.

These people had so much to give. So much more they could do.

Yet, they did nothing. They watched an object called TV all day or played games on another box called a computer or a video game. His world had similar machines, but not for games. Never for games.

"Hello? Are you there?"

Sheesh. "Sorry."

"Look, you called me. Not the other way around. I'm going. You can come or not come. I don't care. I'm going to bed now. See you tomorrow."

"Wait."

She was gone. Damn it. He stared down at the phone in his hand, something else these people appeared to be permanently attached to. Now what had she said? He'd missed part of it. Something about going back and he could come or not. So, she *wasn't* planning on going anywhere tonight?

He understood only so much of the weird innuendos and body language of these people.

Was she going back tonight?

Chapter 5

STOREY WOKE ENERGIZED the next morning. It was Saturday. She planned on going to the mine. By way of her floor – as soon as she figured it out. As much as she'd told Eric he could come, she wasn't planning on telling him about her private entrance.

She grabbed up her favorite pencil and sketchbook. Opening to the right page, she laid it down on the floor. As it hit, something caught her eye. Her heart sped up and she crouched down for a better look. The door in her picture had unlocked itself. She might just be able to get through.

First she had to get dressed. She didn't want to end up in some strange place dressed in nightclothes. After donning jeans, t-shirt and sneakers and brushing her hair, she stood on her bed and considered if she'd forgotten anything. Her backpack was still packed with water and a flashlight along with chalk to mark her locations. She'd get it right this time.

After a few moments pondering the contents, she added her pencil and a smaller sketchbook. And felt like an idiot. If anyone saw her preparing for a trip through her bedroom floor, they'd have her committed.

She stood up, took one deep breath for courage, and jumped.

And went right though the floor.

She came to an abrupt halt in the darkness. Her knees

buckled, sending her to one side. Instead of being afraid, she laughed, joy and relief mixing with a sense of exultation. She wasn't crazy. This wasn't her imagination. She'd really jumped through her floor. No damage. No broken beams or flooring or ceiling.

Just a doorway in her sketch. How amazing was that?

Standing up, Storey searched the darkness, listening for identifiable sounds. She'd thought long and hard about what she'd do once she made it back here. Cocking her head to one side, she realized she could hear…nothing. No sounds of water running down the walls, or mice scrabbling against the ground. Not even a bit of breeze whistling down the tunnels. Nothing.

She clicked on her flashlight sending light slicing through unforgiving darkness. "How could anything be so absent of light and sound?" She frowned. Her voice didn't even echo. Had it last time? Sure it had. Still it was different now? She didn't remember much of her science lessons on light and noise, but thought emptiness helped create the echo effect.

So weird. Standing still, she sent light out as far as it could reach in all directions. Then she checked out the space behind her.

Nothing. No walls shone back on her. Turning the light onto the floor, she studied the flooring and wondered at the smooth look of the planks. So perfect, they didn't appear real. It wasn't what she'd expected.

Then she checked out the ceiling. The light went into endless darkness. If there was a ceiling, it was so high as to be untouchable. She knew she hadn't jumped more than eight feet. Her knees hadn't hurt on landing.

So, if she'd jumped through the same hole and landed in

the same black nothingness, where was the damn door?

Taking out her chalk, she drew a large circle with an X in the middle of it. She wanted to mark her position so she didn't get lost. At least this way if she were to jump again, she'd be able to check that she landed at the same place. She didn't want to consider that she might have ended up somewhere new.

First things first, she needed to find the door. Last time it had been behind her. With her flashlight showing the way, she turned, searching behind her for the door. Last time that first slice of light had appeared to be a long way away. In truth, it hadn't been more than thirty or fifty feet.

She paced off thirty paces and stopped. She couldn't see anything anywhere. Looking behind her, relief swept through her at the X on the floor in the bright beam of light. Good. She just needed to do this systematically. Taking a deep breath, she moved forward another thirty paces. Still nothing showed in her light. Uneasiness squirmed in her stomach. Keep going forward or try a new direction? Deciding to move another thirty steps, she paced again, and then stopped and drew another big X, labeling it number two. Then she backtracked to her original spot and paced ninety paces in the opposite direction. By the time she finished, she'd created a square with four Xs at the corners and a big X in the middle. Not much help, considering she had yet to find a perimeter wall.

She stood in the middle of her markings and puzzled over it. What kind of tunnel could have no walls? Not possible. She tried to visualize the space. It had to be a natural cave to require no support beams or walls. Damn. Why hadn't she brought a bigger flashlight? Annoyance flooded through her. Oh wait, maybe because she didn't have one!

Her cell phone rang. Such an ordinary thing, and so normal in the midst of so much abnormal, its very mundaneness surprised her. How could she get reception in here? "Hello?"

Static filled her ear. Figured. "Hello?"

She tried answering several more times, then clicked it off, returning it to her pocket. A moment later, the musical notes on her phone sounded again. A text. Hmmm. She clicked on it to read the incoming message.

Where the hell are you?

Eric. And pissed.

She answered. *I'm in the mine. I told you to come if you wanted.* After she hit send, she waited, a half grin on her face. He wouldn't take it quietly. Her instinct proved right as a text came right back. *I'm on my way. WAIT.*

"Like I have a choice." She sniffed at his autocratic response. Speaking to the empty space around her she snapped at the missing Eric, "Then hurry up. Where the hell is that door?"

She passed the time by walking out to each of her circles and spent several minutes studying the darkness around her. There appeared to be nothing there. Walking back to the middle, she sat down to wait. Within minutes another text came through. She hopped to her feet. Eric said he was approaching the door. She waited for the welcoming sliver of light. It never came. Nerves bunched as she waited and worried. What if he couldn't open the door? He'd done it once. The wait seemed interminable. She chewed her fingernails as she waited and waited.

Damn it. She sent him another text, reading aloud as her fingers whipped across the keyboard. "What's wrong?"

"I've opened the door. Where are you?"

Shit. She hopped to her feet and spun around looking for the doorway. He wasn't there. Shakes and shivers wracked her slight frame as she realized the enormity of her situation.

She'd landed in a different place.

Eric had come to the rescue. He was at the door to the mine. He'd actually managed to open the locked door again, clearing one of the hurdles she'd worried about, but she wasn't there.

So, where the hell was she?

ERIC STOOD IN the doorway. "Storey? Storey, are you here? Where are you?"

Leaving the door wide open, Eric stepped inside and took a long look around. He could see the back wall. There was no sign of her. "Shit." Where had she gone?

A horrible thought surfaced. She couldn't have jumped elsewhere. She didn't know how. At least he didn't think she did. No, she'd said she was here. So, this is where she *thought* she was.

"Storey?"

No answer. Could she have gotten out? He pulled out his phone. Her incoming text asked where he was. Double shit.

Where was she? And how could he find her?

Paxton. Using his codex, he coded in the notes that would allow him to cross the veil where he stood. In seconds he breathed the air of his own world. After a quick glance around, he headed for Paxton's office.

"Finally." Buried in books, eyeglasses perched on the

bridge of his nose, Paxton snorted at him. "Your father has been asking about you. I do hope you have the stylus with you."

"We've got a problem." Eric raced to the holograph screens. "Storey jumped again. Only she's gone somewhere else this time and I can't find her."

Paxton came running, his long midnight blue robes flapping in the wind. "Oh dear! This is exactly what we were trying to avoid. We can't just have a human running loose on our side. There's no knowing what kind of chaos she could create."

"She's not trying to cause any trouble." Storey was curious, not a terrorist. Eric was compelled to defend her. "She thinks she's in the same place as last time, but I just checked and she's not there."

"That's because she's here. She's jumped to Stanshor mine!" Paxton tapped one of the screens on the left.

Eric peered closer. Sure enough Storey stood in the middle of a different portal. "What? How could she have made it there?"

"The stylus. It's trying to go home. That's the closest jump to the science hall."

"How would the stylus know that?"

"Through its ancient memories. It's taking her where it wants to go. You have to get her back to Bankhead Mine."

Eric snorted. "And how do you expect me to do that? She's a thousand miles in the wrong direction." He fisted his hands on his hips and snorted at the monitor. How the hell had she done that?

"Jump with her."

"She'll know," Eric warned.

"Not if you do it right. Jump at the doorway. From one

to the other. If you catch it right, she won't even know what the world outside of Stanshor looks like."

Crap. "That's a lot of 'ifs.'" He rubbed his temple, trying to work through the process.

"Too bad. If you can't keep her under control then you have to clean up her messes." Paxton motioned behind him. "Use the doorway in my office. You can dial up Stanshor, then let her out like she's expecting you to."

"Right. Good luck with that," he muttered the last under his breath, loving the new expressions he'd been picking up on the other side. And they were so apt. Storey wasn't stupid. She'd know something was up.

Eric walked into Paxton's office, wondering what he was going to say to her. If he let her know what she'd done was illegal in his world he could kiss his career goodbye. Keeping her in the dark was going to be even harder.

He set the coordinates for Stanshor and walked through Paxton's doorway to the entrance of Stanshor Mine. The development here was at least ten times bigger than the one in Bankhead. If she'd gotten lost in here, it could take days to find her. And that's if he knew where to start.

The door was locked as per standard practice. Using his soulkey, honored with the highest security, he unlocked the mine door. Taking a deep breath, he pushed it open. He could only hope she was there.

He stepped inside, careful to keep the door partially closed so she couldn't see out.

"There you are. What took so long?"

Her voice, sharp and stressed, snapped out at him. Temper? Or something else. Bemused, Eric could only watch as she strode toward him, backpack in hand. He partially closed the door behind him. He couldn't have her escaping until he'd made the changes. "Well, hi. How are you? Nice of you to come and rescue me. Sorry for being such an idiot and jumping into a cave again without anyone knowing."

Good. The sarcasm in his voice garnered him a disgusted look as she went to brush past him. Past him? Shit. He spun to close the door.

Her hand wrapped around his arm, a last grasp from a dying person. "I have to get out." A shudder rippled down her and she sucked air through her clenched teeth. Her eyes stared toward the crack of light. Eric studied her finely etched features and narrowed his gaze.

She was headed for a panic attack. He had to get her out of here and fast. Shit. The timing had to be perfect. "Let me go first." Not giving her a chance to argue, he stepped in front of her and strode the short distance to the door. Using his codex, Eric shifted the locations until the entrance to Bankhead Mine stood outside and not the entrance to Stanshor Mine. He'd never done this type of shift before. How long would his luck hold?

"I have to get outside." Storey burst past him, her voice tight, flat.

Crap. He grabbed her arm and tugged her back. She spun around and ended up in his arms. Huge chocolate eyes, so close to his own, widened in confusion. It's not what he'd planned but…he couldn't help himself. He lowered his head and swallowed her startled response with a quick kiss at the same time as he pushed down on the transporter button.

At least it was supposed to be quick. And he hadn't meant it to be hot. At least not that hot. He'd aimed for warmer than friends and cooler than lovers. Instead, sparks flew as flames licked across his skin, burning, searing the taste of her, the feel of her in his arms, forever in his mind.

He shuddered. *Step back. Danger.* It wasn't supposed to be like this. Eric pulled back, struggling for air. Storey stared up at him, her eyes the color of molten chocolate, confusion swirling in their depths.

"Hey." His voice wavered, just a bit. He recognized it. Thought she might have too. He cleared this throat. "That was an *I'm just glad to see you alive* kiss. Sorry it got a little out of hand. I was afraid you'd be lost in there forever." Turning her gently, he nudged her out into her world. She was dangerous. She'd wreak havoc if left on her own in his dimension. She was already wreaking havoc. With his heart.

Chapter 6

STOREY WANTED TO look back on this moment and be proud that she'd acted like Eric's kiss hadn't just blown every other kiss out the water. In fact, she now knew she hadn't been kissed before. At least not properly.

Yeah, Eric knew how to kiss.

Come on, Storey, you can do this. Act natural and, for heaven's sake, close your mouth and quit gawking.

She forced a smile and lifted her face to the sky. Surely, he couldn't know about the tumultuous flutter of her heart or stomach. And the shudders wracking her spine were on the inside and not something he could see. She stole a glance his way, grateful he was checking out the entrance to Bankhead Mine and thankful she was outside and not still locked inside. She took several gulps of fresh air and closed her eyes, waiting for her senses to return to normal.

Why had he kissed her? And why like that? Or had the second part been a surprise for him, too? God, she hoped so. To think her reaction had been one-sided would be one of life's nastiest jokes.

Sensing his gaze, she opened her eyes. His blue eyes studied her. With a nonchalance she didn't feel, she said, "I didn't realize how wonderful fresh air smells and how warming, how healing, the sun is."

Pursing his lips, he gave her an understanding nod. "After being locked in a mine twice, that's understandable. The real question is – was the experience bad enough to stop you from repeating it?" He waggled his eyebrows and hooked his arm through hers. "Come on. I have to get home."

"Oh?" She shrugged. Trying to put more distance between her and that dynamite kiss she added, "I thought I'd stay and explore some more."

He grunted. "Damn good thing I closed the door then, isn't it? Does the law matter to you at all?" His voice rose in exasperation.

He grabbed her shoulders, spinning her around until she couldn't miss the sign in front of them. "Can you read that? No Trespassing." He snorted at her. "Is that simple enough? This is private property. You can't just wander around here. It's dangerous."

She stood toe-to-toe against him and glared.

"I got it. Except I'm not a kid anymore and I can make my own decisions. Something weird is going on and I'm going to figure out what it is. You don't like it. Fine. You don't have to get involved." That he was right wasn't enough to make her stop. She had to sort this out. She could hardly forget the whole thing happened, could she? "Thanks for helping me. Go on and enjoy your don't-rock-the-boat existence."

She stepped back and took a look around. "I wish you'd tell me how to open the damn door." At his look, she added, "Not going to happen, huh? Fine." She threw her backpack over her shoulder. "Thanks. I can manage on my own."

She strode off in the direction of home, her head and heart a mess. Then she came to a sudden stop. Spinning back around, she asked, "Where were you earlier? When you texted to say you had the door open and where was I?"

He shrugged, a sheepish look on his face. "I wasn't here yet. I thought the scare might stop you from playing these dangerous games."

She gasped. "That's so mean." She strode off, almost running to get away from him. How could he have done something like that? And then there was that damn kiss. Why did he mess with her feelings so badly? Whatever. She didn't intend to spend time with him anyway.

The sun shone bright and warm, helping to chase away the last of the uneasiness lingering in her mind. The panic had subsided and the anger had burned through the rest of her nervousness. She took a deep breath and sighed.

Strong arms grabbed from behind.

Eric spun her around until she stood facing him. A very pissed off Eric. So why did she have to notice how anger lit the deep blue in his eyes and hollowed out his face, high-lighting the strength of his jaw bones? She did so love the dimple in his chin.

"Are you always so disagreeable?"

She raised one eyebrow and refused to back down.

"I guess that means yes, huh?" His jaw clenched as he glared down at her.

Odd how nice it was to look up at a guy. "That's not fair. You don't know everything that's gone on. You're judging me without having all the information."

"Then talk. Explain it to me." He stepped back and crossed his arms, waiting.

She snorted then shifted to look up at the sky. She shouldn't have brought it up. What to tell him? How much would he believe? No one would believe everything. "I don't know how much to tell you."

"Everything." There it was again, that dominant, implacable wall.

She sighed and tucked her hair behind her ear. "You won't believe me."

"Try me."

There just wasn't any give in him. "This might take some time."

"I have all the time we need."

"Really?" she challenged. "I thought you had to go home."

"I'll make my excuses later."

She grimaced. Of course he would. "Fine. But I want to sit down somewhere first."

"Over there."

She checked out where he pointed. Several large rocks sat under the boughs of a blue spruce. "Okay. But don't blame me if this all sounds a little farfetched," she warned.

He sat down, crossed those long legs of his and waited.

She frowned. "I don't know where to start."

"At the beginning."

Well, duh. She sat back and took a deep breath. "Several days ago, well maybe a week now. I don't know. The days have whipped by so fast." She chewed her bottom lip, trying to understand how that had happened.

"And," he prompted.

"I found a pencil. That weird one you asked about."

"Where?"

He said it so abruptly she paused, thrown off track. It took her a moment. "On the way to school, I walked through the park and saw it by a rock at the side of the creek. Just lying there."

There'd been a sense that she'd been destined to find it. That she had a connection with it. Not that she was going to tell him that. "Anyways, I've always done artwork of some kind, only…after getting that pencil, it's like I've been obsessed." She slid a sidelong glance his way. "I mean really obsessed. I don't notice when I'm drawing, but it's like I go into a trance or something. I cover every available space on any page. Sometimes, it's just doodles and other times it's really cool stuff. One of the drawings was a door."

Eric leaned closer, his eyes narrowing at her words. "What kind of door?"

She shrugged. "It was scrunched up, so I redrew it on a clean sheet."

She paused.

"And?" Impatience prodded him up off the rocks to pace around before coming back to crouch down in front of her. "What happened next?"

Storey puzzled over his attitude. But she'd started so she might as well carry on. "I got mad one day because the drawings wouldn't leave me alone. They wanted me to draw, draw and draw some more. I felt like I was losing it. Or that they were controlling me." She took a deep breath. "I threw the book down on the floor in my room. I had been on my bed and I was so frustrated, so angry…I don't know…anyways I stomped on it…and that's when things got even weirder."

"Weirder?" His gaze caught hers and held on. She couldn't break the link, it was so intense. "How?"

She took a deep breath. "When I jumped onto my book, I went through my bedroom floor. One simple hop off my bed and I ended up inside Bankhead Mine."

SO, THAT WAS it. Eric sat back, stunned at the sheer

simplicity of the steps that led to her crossing the veil and entering his world. At the same time, it scared the hell out of him. If it happened once, or twice in this case, it could happen anytime with anyone. Not good. If anyone else had picked the stylus up, the stylus probably would have remained dormant. However, with Storey being an artist, an open young mind, the stylus had a perfect tool to get it home.

He studied Storey's face. She'd dropped her gaze to the rocks at her feet. Ashamed? She appeared to be over her panic attack and now sat looking curiously embarrassed. He still had trouble reading her facial expressions.

"So, now that I've told you, I'm heading home." She sent him a quick uncertain glance before hopping off the big rock.

"Wait."

Hesitating, she stalled, her back to him. "What now?"

"I believe you." He walked around to stand in front of her.

The impatience drained from her face as hope filled her eyes. "You do? Really?"

"Yes."

They stood and looked at each other for a long moment, the beginning of acceptance sparking between them.

"Don't suppose you'd care to demonstrate, would you?" Eric asked.

A half frown crossed her face. She glanced at the sky and then back at him. "Only if you know how to unlock the damn door from the inside."

Right. That's how she'd gotten out both times – he'd helped her. He looked back the way they'd come, his mind spinning with possibilities. "Maybe."

"Maybe, isn't good enough. I don't relish the idea of being stuck in there any longer than I was today." She continued in a barely audible voice, "And preferably not that long."

"Can I see the book and the pencil, if you don't mind?"

She studied his face. "I suppose that's okay. We have to go to my house then."

He motioned toward the path and grinned. "After you."

STOREY DIDN'T KNOW how she'd ended up so involved with Eric. Every time she turned around – there he was. If only the other girls could see her now. Not that they'd believe their eyes. They'd barely believed it when she dated Jeff. Still, her heart lurched at the thought of her old boyfriend. He'd wanted her to move on. *He* certainly had. The corner of her mouth drooped.

"Tell me what happened today."

Presuming he meant the jump to the mine, she explained the series of events that led up to getting lost again. "I thought I could find the door on my own this time." She took several more steps, before continuing. "I paced off specific distances and marked the floor with chalk to stop me from getting lost." She shrugged carelessly. "Somehow, it didn't work out that way."

"Plans rarely do." The cryptic tone of his voice confused her. Studying his face didn't give her a clue to his thoughts.

At her front door, she stopped. Who was home? It was Saturday, so her mom would be home. Annalea, her assistant, would be minding the store again today. "My mom is here."

"Is that a problem?"

She groaned. "All the time, just not for the reason you might think."

"Oh?"

Refusing to answer, Storey opened the front door.

"Storey? Where have you been? I thought I'd let you sleep in only to find you weren't even in bed—" Her mom, dressed in her typical lounging pant set, stopped her all-out flight down the stairs as her gaze landed on Eric. Flustered, she finished descending and fluffed her hair.

Storey rolled her eyes.

"Hi. I'm Storey's mother. Nice to meet you."

Eric smiled down at her. "I'm Eric. A friend of Storey's."

Stepping back, Storey watched the two interact. No surprise registered in Eric's voice or face as he looked at her Wiccan mother. But then he might not know about her religious beliefs. Wasn't this an important weekend for her, too? In the back of her mind, nearly forgotten under the weird mine stuff, the memory of her mom mentioning a special ceremony poked at her.

"How nice. Please come in. Storey, where were you this morning?"

Storey stiffened slightly. "Same as yesterday. I woke up early and walked through the park with my sketchbook. I met Eric there."

"I wish you'd told me or left me a message. I don't like waking up to find you gone."

"Sorry, Mom. You were still asleep, and I didn't want to wake you." Storey brushed past her and headed up the stairs. "I'm just going to show Eric some of my art. We don't have much time – he's expected back at his house."

"Oh." Her mother smiled at Eric. "In that case. She's very talented, you know."

"I've noticed."

Storey watched from the landing as Eric smiled at her mom, then she took the stairs two at a time. He followed her up. At the top landing, he glanced at her, a questioning look in his eyes. "Problems?"

"No." She led the way to her room.

At her doorway, she paused. Had she put her underwear away? How humiliating if she hadn't. With a grimace and a deep breath for courage, she flung the door wide and stepped inside. Her sketchbook lay on the floor, just as she'd left it. Pointing it out, she stood back and watched him approach it. One thing was for sure, from the care he took with the sketch, he might actually believe her.

She couldn't help leaning back against the wall, a little stunned at the realization that she had a guy in her bedroom. Wow. Kind of cool. Then again, she was behind the times. Many girls at school were already having sex. Of course, there were those with parents who would freak if they saw a guy in their daughter's bedroom, too. Her mom had let Eric waltz right in.

"So where's the stylus?"

"Stylus? You mean the pencil?" Why would he call it that?

"Right. Where is it?"

"In my bag." She slid the bag off her shoulder and pulled the ties open. Rummaging through, she remembered that she'd stuffed the pencil in her pocket. Pulling it out, she handed it to him.

He snatched it up, then dropped it immediately. "Ouch." It landed on the floor and rolled several feet.

"What is your problem?" She scrambled to pick it up. "It's a pencil, not a knife or a bomb." Straightening, she sat down and held it out for him again. His response was tentative at best. Narrowing her eyes, she watched him grasp it as if the stupid thing was going to bite him. She had to admit seeing it in his hand made her nervous, like she was in danger of losing something precious. After a tense moment, she said, "Hand it over."

"What?" He stared, mesmerized. "Awesome pencil. I'd love to have one myself."

Something about the way he said it made her uneasy. Yeah, he'd like to have one, but not a different one, he wanted hers.

"Now."

He looked up at her, his jaw line firming, squaring as if fighting himself over her demand. For a moment she wasn't sure he was going to give the pencil back, then he tossed it her way. As her fingers closed around it, relief coursed through her. Now she knew how that old hobbit had felt in the Lord of the Rings movie when he got back the ring. She frowned at the whimsical thought. Except this wasn't a magical pencil.

A light bulb went off in her head.

She was an idiot…because that's exactly what it was. The pencil had to be magic. How else could she walk through a sketch? She couldn't, unless she'd used something special to make it.

"Where's the blow up picture you did?"

Startled, Storey tried to focus on Eric now standing in front of her.

Storey pointed out the book off to the left on her computer desk. He picked it up and made a weird sound.

"You're acting really strange, you know that?"

"Am not." He turned the pages, studying each intently,

his face filled with conflicting emotions. Something about his demeanor made her uneasy. His stare struck her as too intense, his spine too stiff, his attention too focused. She kept her eyes trained on him as he meticulously checked out her book.

He sucked in his breath, the color draining from his cheeks. After a long moment he spun to stare at her, his eyes gone the color of obsidian. "When did you draw this one?"

"Last night. After we talked. I actually haven't taken a look at it since." She leaned forward, but was at the wrong angle to see it clearly.

Eric stared at her in horror and started whispering some kind of weird chant. She'd heard plenty of spells being cast over the last few years, yet she'd never heard anything like what he was speaking. "Are you a Wiccan?" she asked curiously, when he took a breath.

Pale and shaking, he shook his head. His voice hoarse, he said, "You have no idea what you've done."

"*I've done?* I haven't done anything." So much for his understanding. He didn't look well. As a matter of fact, he looked closer to passing out than anyone she'd ever seen before. "Are you okay? You look like you're going to faint."

"Faint?" he cried out in horror.

"Hey, chill. I don't want my mom running up here."

He sank down on the bed beside her, shaking his head. "I'm trying to keep my voice down. You're a little tough on my ego."

Storey closed her eyes and prayed for patience. "Ego? You are one weird guy, you know that?" Opening her eyes, she stared at his stunned, almost devastated eyes. "Okay, please explain. What is going on? Why are you upset and what do you think I've done?"

In a hushed, thick voice, he said, "Unleashed thousands of demons from the world in between."

Storey stared at him. *Figures.* She'd finally met a guy who seemed to like her, was a dynamite kisser and sure enough he had looney tunes playing away inside his head. "Huh? What did you say?" She shook her head. "No wait. Never mind. Look…" She stood up and walked to the door, opening it. "It's gotta be time for your medicine or something. It's definitely time for you to go home."

He stared at her with empty eyes. She started to freak a little. "Did you hear me? You need to go home. You said you were supposed to earlier and I understand now. No problem. I won't tell anyone. Just…please go."

With a shake of his head, he stood up. "I can't do that. I need you to meet someone."

Storey shook her head. "No way. I'm *so* not going to meet any of the people in your life."

"Look I'm not sick. I don't need medicine. I need you to understand that this pencil, this stylus is special. It creates doorways – as you've found out. Somehow, you've opened a door that has remained sealed for hundreds of years. Even I don't understand the repercussions here. But," he emphasized, "we have to fix this."

"Fix what? I don't understand. You aren't making any sense."

"Like what you told me earlier down by the mine made sense?" He closed his eyes briefly. "You trusted me to listen to you and now I'm asking you to listen to me. The stylus enhances your abilities. In your hand it can create doorways." His blue eyes opened to blaze down at her. "Please. It won't take long. We could be there and back in an hour. I need you to show these drawings to someone."

Peering into his eyes, Storey wondered how to tell if someone was late for his dose of anti-psychotics. "Where?"

"Not far."

"Not far doesn't mean much."

"This is important. Vitally important. Please. What harm could it do to talk to him?"

He reached out and grasped her hand. Staring deep into her eyes, he pleaded, "Please. We have to go show him this." He flipped the sketchbook around so she could see the picture. A picture on a different page.

"Show him what? That's just something I drew before falling asleep last night. I was doodling on the door."

"Look at it closer," he ordered.

Playing along, she took another look. The markings looked different. She realized the doorway stood slightly ajar. Just then Eric shifted his fingers and she could see the picture clearer.

There, wrapped around the wood, as if trying to force it wider open, were eight long, knobby fingers.

THE MOMENT HE felt the shift in her attitude, his panic eased. At least most of it. "Thank you." He stepped back, rotating his neck and shoulders as the tension eased.

"I didn't say I'd go."

"Yes, you did." He closed her sketchbook. "Let's go. Now." As much as he wanted to take the stylus from her, it was clear that it had already bonded, and the person who'd tried to take it from her had better watch out.

"Wait. What's the rush? Besides, what am I going to tell my mother?"

"We'll explain that you forgot your homework and that I

have the assignment that you're missing."

"That's great for you. I don't do homework."

He shot her a look of disgust. "Then you should. Do you really just want to work at the corner store all your life?"

"I *don't* work at a corner store," she snapped.

"No, but that's all you're going to be good for with your education level, isn't it." Thank heavens for the comprehensive database they kept on the humans. His studies had allowed for a unique insight to Storey and the society she lived in.

"Arrgh. Who are you to talk?"

She stormed downstairs. The chanting reached them first. Right, preparations for the ceremony. Rather than disturbing them, Storey and Eric made a quick exit out the back door. Eric's pace picked up outside. He practically ran – back in the direction of the damn mine. When they reached the edge of Lewis Park and where she'd told him about the portal, she'd had enough.

"What the hell are we doing back here?" She glared at him and backed up several feet. "We're almost back to where we started."

"We're probably close enough." He dug into his pocket and grabbed a weird silver bracelet that he clasped around his wrist. He tapped a series of buttons on it, filling the air with a musical set of notes.

Story narrowed her eyes at him. "What's that?" she asked suspiciously. "I've never seen anything like it."

"No, it's not common over here."

"Over here?" She surveyed the deserted park and the overgrown path that led to the mine entrance. How come in all the years she'd lived here, she'd never once gone down the path to the mine?

"Yes, over here." He grinned, reached out and grabbed her hand. "Just a few more steps. Here."

Spluttering her protests, she snapped, "I don't want to go with you anymore. I've decided I don't like you. You're beyond irritating, you know that."

A strange voice interjected. "No, he doesn't, but the rest of us do."

Chapter 7

S TOREY SPUN AROUND. Her jaw dropped. "Where'd you come from?" she demanded, her eyes locked on the costume-clad man now before her. "You weren't here a second ago."

Her voice rose to a loud gasp and her eyes widened as the wall behind him came into focus. She gulped and spun in a circle. The sky had disappeared. Leaves no longer crunched under her feet and the fresh woodsy scent no longer drifted her way. Her stomach wiggled, then wiggled some more as she gulped for air. Where was she? And how had she gotten here?

They'd been standing beside the creek then…a shudder snapped from her toes to her head with realization. Swallowing hard, she shifted closer to Eric.

The wizened old man with a huge beard and tufts of hair decorating his bald head glared at her. His gaze switched to Eric. "What have you done? Do you know how many rules you've broken?" His voice rose to a high pitched squeak at the end. His hands, fisted on his hips, all but disappeared into the folds of his robes.

Storey studied the angry character in front of her. The angle of his chin, that aristocratic nose tilt, that demanding voice – yeah, he was used to giving orders. And expecting them to be carried out. He was a little out of her experience.

She couldn't help asking, "Who are you?"

A piercing blue gaze landed on her and narrowed. "I'm Paxton. And you're Storey Dalton." The gaze shifted to Eric. "Explain."

Eric opened his mouth. No words came out.

"Now." The bright blue gaze hardened to steel. When Eric didn't immediately jump in with an explanation, he added, "You're done. You know that, don't you?"

"I had to," Eric protested. "You don't understand."

"No. I don't." Paxton spread his arms wide. "I can't until you explain."

Eric glanced over at Storey. "Let me have the sketchbook, please."

She gazed at him for a long moment, not fully understanding yet knowing it was important. She handed it over. Her stomach knotted as Eric flipped through the pages, searching for what he wanted. He went too far and had to go back a few pages, letting out a small hiss as he did so.

"Here." He twisted the book and placed it under Paxton's nose.

Paxton's eyes widened. Glancing from Storey to Eric then back again at the picture, he asked, "How?"

"Show him," Eric said to her.

Reaching into her pocket, Storey pulled out her pencil or stylus, as Eric called it, and held it up.

The color leached from Paxton's face and he took a small step back. "No. Oh, no."

"Oh, yes."

"What?" Storey was beyond confused and she had no explanation for the coldness in her stomach. Ice had spread out to her limbs. Wrapping her arms around her belly, she wished she knew what the hell was going on. "Look, I don't understand. What's wrong with that picture? It's just a sketch. It's not real or anything."

"Did you draw this picture?" At Storey's nod, Paxton continued, "With…that?" He pointed to the pencil.

Again she nodded. He closed his eyes and started speaking in some weird language. The same one Eric had used earlier.

"Do you guys belong to the some religious group where you speak in tongues or something? I've never heard a language quite like that."

"You mock us?" shrieked Paxton, stiffening in outrage. "Do you realize what you have done?"

"Obviously not," she snapped. "Since no one will tell me what the hell is going on."

Eric's eyes widened. He stared at her wordlessly.

She glared at Eric, catching his wince before he covered it up. "Now what?"

"We don't swear here. It's considered rude," Eric whispered. "Paxton doesn't know that word but anyone who's studied your language might."

"Rude? I'm supposed to worry about my manners now? What the hell are you talking about? Over where?"

He spluttered. "Please, show some respect. Don't swear."

"All right, geeze." His look didn't improve. "Oh, for crying out loud. Geeze is *not* a swear word." She glowered at him. What was his problem, anyway? And since when had he become such a prude?

Paxton's cheeks sucked in like small craters.

"Whatever." She held out her hand. "I'll take my sketchbook now, thanks." Hand outstretched, she snapped her fingers when Eric didn't pass it over. "I don't know what game you're playing, and I don't care. I want no part of it.

So, I'm going home."

"No, you're not." Paxton drew up to his full height. Storey's gaze widened as he stretched above her. How tall was he?

"You'll stay in our world until we get to the bottom of this."

"Your world," she snapped. "What are you talking about?"

"You are…" Eric paused…took a deep breath…then rushed to get the rest of the sentence out. "You are in another dimension."

"Oh, for the love of God." Storey threw up her hands at the stony looks shooting her way. "Look, I've had enough. You zip me to another dimension, whatever that means, without asking my permission, tell me I can't go home, give no explanation as to what is going on and then expect me to be calm about it!"

Eric reached out a reassuring hand. She stumbled back out of range. "No." She pointed at Paxton and said, "Hell, no."

This time, Eric grabbed her shoulder and gave her a good shake. Glaring down at her, he said, "Stop. I know you don't understand. Just, please, calm down. I *will* explain." He glanced over at the steaming Paxton. "I promise."

Storey stepped back, glaring up at him. "You'd better. And for your information, I swear when I'm pissed off, so don't piss me off. That includes shaking me."

He closed his eyes briefly, dropped his hand and stepped away. "You'd make a saint crazy," he muttered.

Paxton gasped in outrage. "Which you aren't," he roared. "You should be able to control this…this female."

"Control," she gasped in shock. For some reason the

whole mess slid from bad into ludicrous. "I must be having a bad dream. Eric? Control me? I don't think so." She started to giggle.

"Oh, thank you very much. See how she treats me?" He scowled at Paxton. "Why did you have to go and say that?"

"That's enough from both of you. This is no laughing matter. We have a crisis on our hands and need to find a solution." He glanced down at the sketchbook now in his hands. "Quickly. Wait in my office while I call an emergency Council meeting."

Storey was still giggling as they took several more steps, then she stopped. This wasn't just a room. This was some kind of laboratory. Stunned, she could only stare at the pristine white counters, walls, ceilings, even the huge monitors were white with a black trim. "Eric?"

"You're in my world now. It's very similar to yours." He hooked his arm through hers. "Don't panic. Everything is fine. I walked you across a veil that exists between the two worlds."

"Veil?" Easy for him to say. Getting her head wrapped around the concept, not so easy. Still, there was no arguing that she walked on tiles and under some kind of weird fluorescent lights instead of grass and sky. "You're not from my world?"

"Nope." As she stopped in front of a large series of monitors, Eric added by way of an explanation. "It's Paxton's communications center. He controls the crossings."

"There's more than one?" She slid him a sideways look. "Does my side know about your side?"

He pursed his lips and shook his head. "We don't think so, but it's possible. There are several crossings; we keep most of them shut down. We travel to your side when we have specific research to complete. To the best of our knowledge, there aren't any crossings from your side to ours – at least not regulated ones."

"So, I'm the first to visit?" For some reason that concept tickled her. She'd always wanted to get away from her life. Now she was in the most bizarre, abnormal situation imaginable and didn't know what to think. Contrary was her name. She should be scared, but it was as if the jumps into the mine had prepared her for this eventuality. Well, not quite *this* reality. Then his words penetrated. They'd been coming to her world whenever they wanted to – yet no one at home knew.

"Come this way." Eric tugged her arm, leading her toward a closed door. She followed, trying to take in everything. So similar and yet…different.

Eric looked normal enough. Paxton didn't. He was a little on the odd side. Then again, what if a monk, Goth or a Muslim person came here? Eric's people would consider him representative of her world, too. "This isn't fair. You know how to do all this and we don't."

"Fair?" Paxton ran up behind them. "Look what happens when you do know a little bit." He brushed past and through the door ahead of them.

"Really." She exhaled heavily. "Let's not forget who left a stylus in my world in the first place. I wouldn't have found it if you'd stayed where you belong." She wasn't going to take the blame for this – whatever *this* was. They shouldn't have sneaked over to her side. Having perpetrated one wrong, they shouldn't have compounded it by leaving something dangerous behind.

"I know."

"Come, come. Don't dawdle. We don't have time. Everyone is almost here." Paxton hurried ahead of them, tossing an urgent look back their way.

Storey didn't get it. "How did everyone manage to get here in the time it took me to walk the length of the floor?"

"Things are a bit different here." He grinned down at her. "You'll see."

"That's what I'm afraid of," she muttered. "Some info would be helpful. Does everyone look like you and Paxton, for a start? I don't want to walk into that room and find talking alligators or some such thing."

He laughed. "No, we all look like you. Although, we call ourselves Torans. And Paxton is a little more unique than the rest of us."

"Is that what you call it?"

Eric stopped at the doorway, twisting to look down on her. "You're stalling. You can do this. Heck, I even went to school and attended classes with you. How bad can this be?"

Glaring at him, she stormed through the doorway and came to a sudden halt on the other side. "No one ever smiles in your world, do they?"

The normal looking room was full. Crowding around a large oval table in the middle of the room were dozens of people and even more stood in the back. Everyone stared, frowning at her. Too bad. Her dreams of a magical world spiriting her away went up in smoke. They all looked depressingly normal.

"They aren't that bad." Eric stepped forward. Staring ahead, his back straight, he addressed the room formally. "Greetings, Council. May I present Storey Dalton. She's from the other side of the veil."

Storey couldn't help stiffening at the multitude of curious and judgmental looks zeroing in on her.

"So I understand," answered a rotund looking man at the head of the table. So round and short, he took up almost two chairs yet could barely rest his arms on the table. And his face…she shuddered. Beady eyes stared out from between the fat rolls with a power that defied description. "And apparently you are responsible for bringing her here?"

Eric's voice deepened. "That's right, father. I felt it best."

Father? Storey glanced between the two men, but didn't recognize any family resemblance. One height challenged and the other height gifted. The change in Eric's voice, however, yeah, there was that whole parent relationship mess between them.

"And just how do you think breaking our rules, rules which have held for centuries, I might add, as now being for the 'best?'"

Eric opened his mouth to explain, when Paxton stepped in. "We don't have time to sort out his punishment right now. We have something much bigger to deal with."

"Punishment? You're going to punish him for bringing me here?" Storey couldn't contain her outrage. Whether she wanted to be here or not, she knew Eric believed he'd done the right thing. "In that case, you can send me home. I'm not going to help if he's in trouble over this." It was all she could do to refrain from swearing. If they pissed her off more, then all bets were off.

"Shh. It's all right. I won't be punished."

His father grunted. "We'll make that decision without any input from you. Breaking the law is a very serious offense. It's not like in your world, young lady. We care about doing the right thing here."

"It's hardly admirable that you sit here and criticize my world when you've been sneaking in and out, taking whatever you want, for centuries. That's called stealing in my world. We'll have this discussion after my people's scientists come over here for several hundred years and steal what they want from you," she snapped in outrage. She strode several steps forward and stood with her hands on her hips, anger vibrating up her back. How dare they?

"Uh, oh," murmured Eric. He stepped up beside her as if bracing for a mortal blow.

The temperature in the room dropped.

Paxton rose and came running over to stand in front of her. "That's enough. She doesn't understand our ways. In this case, I believe Eric was right to do what he did."

A murmur rustled throughout the room. To have stood beside her, siding with her…had to be big. Storey didn't care how big. She hadn't been a conformist in her world, she wasn't about to start now.

The breath wooshed out of Eric and his shoulders relaxed.

"Eric, take her over to the seats so we can get started."

Storey noticed the two empty chairs only when Eric motioned toward them. Paxton waited until they'd sat down before addressing the swelling crowd. "Now. This problem is one for both our worlds. Several weeks ago a research team, Denby's team, I believe, crossed over. They were there for less than an hour when Sarcov, the head scientist, became sick. We think at this point he might have been allergic to some of the plants he was studying."

Eric shifted. Storey shot him a questioning look. He never took his gaze off Paxton.

"…in the panic to treat him and get him home, the team missed packing up some equipment. As a result, his stylus was lost."

The murmur in the room swelled. Paxton held up his hand. "I know. I know. We weren't made aware of this until Sarcov woke up in the hospital and asked for it." He looked around the room. "We sent a team back immediately. And they were almost upon it when they saw a young girl stoop to pick it up. They followed her, hoping to recover the instrument, only they lost her in the school." He nodded toward Storey. "This is the girl."

He stopped to pin the seated members with a cutting glare, before saying, "What's important to understand is that she picked it up with her bare hands and had no problem in doing so."

Over the growing murmur of excited voices, Paxton glanced over at Storey. "I'll explain in a minute."

"Storey didn't know what she'd found. As an artist, she was happy with her find, thinking it was only a writing instrument. Except she soon found herself driven to draw on every surface from her textbooks, homework, even her own arms."

Storey pulled her sleeves down over her wrists. Her fingers clenched in her lap. She hadn't thought he'd noticed. She'd tried to wash it off, but no go.

Eric interjected. "Sorry, Storey. I didn't say anything to you because I didn't want to make you uncomfortable." He turned back to address the elders. "She was listening to the stylus. It's been trying to come back home."

His father shook his head. "That's not possible. She's not capable of hearing the stylus. They speak only to their owners."

Paxton shook his head. "It *shouldn't* be possible. However, as we've never lost anything over there, we don't *know* what's possible and what's not. Especially with something soulbound."

Eric's father's gaze narrowed, sharpened. "Doesn't that defy the term?"

Another seated elder spoke. "Exactly. If the stylus was soulbound, how did she manage to pick it up?"

"We're not sure of anything in this case. It's possible," Paxton suggested, "that due to Sarcov's illness, the bond between him and the stylus weakened. It's also possible that crossing the veil changed something that contributed to the bond weakening. The stylus might have been able to detach." Paxton shrugged. "We just don't know."

Murmurs rose through the crowd.

Paxton straightened and raised his right hand, commanding silence from the audience. "We don't have all the answers here. There are much more important issues to focus on. We know that Storey picked up the stylus and used it for her artwork. However, without knowing what she was doing, she drew a doorway and actually managed to go through it, thus entering our world."

The crowd cried out in shock. "What? She came here? Without us knowing?"

"Yes, that's correct. Except the monitoring system tracked her movements."

Storey leaned toward Eric, her eyes widening in shock. "I have?"

"Yes. The mine is partially on our side."

She blinked. Then blinked again. "So, when I went through the floor in my bedroom and ended up in the mine, that was the same as crossing the veil?"

He studied her face then grinned, that same lopsided smile. Damn, he shouldn't be allowed to do that.

"Something like that. The stylus actually took you to a

formal crossing zone in the mine. You couldn't get out because it wasn't active on our side. It's only because the crossing notified Paxton of your activity that you were found at all."

Dismay crossed her face. "Are you saying I might have never gotten out?"

"If we didn't monitor the veil then yes. It's quite likely you'd have died there and no one would have known." He reached across to cover her clenched hands with his. "However, Paxton *did* find you. He told me and I opened the door on your side of the world to let you out."

"And the second time I went in?" Storey struggled to understand.

Eric grimaced. "The stylus took you to a different gate entirely, presumably because the first attempt didn't work. I had to make it look like Bankhead mine when you walked out." He tilted his head, this time a glint of amusement in his eyes. "I also have a soulkey that unlocks almost anything. It has a few other functions that are dangerous to use if you are untrained."

The mine door. Storey shook her head and laughed. "No way. That's not possible. How could I not notice?"

He flushed then mumbled, "I did it while you were…distracted."

She blinked. Memories flooded in. That kiss. That hot, wonderful, mind-blowing kiss. "That's why you kissed me?" she hissed. "Oh, my God."

Eric's face slipped from the color of a sun-kissed peach color to a fat ripe tomato. Storey glanced around, noting multiple disapproving frowns deepened as they understood, too. "Oh crap. Sorry everyone. Swearing is common in my world. It's not an insult against humanity over there."

"It's not over here either; however, it is a sign of disrespect," said another older male, this one just as disapproving as the others at the table.

"Right." She grimaced. "I'll try to remember that."

Paxton took control of the conversation again, lowering the noise level in the room instantly. "The real problem is that Storey drew something else." Paxton reached for Storey's sketchbook sitting in front of him on the table. "This."

He flipped through the book until he found the right page, then held it up to show everyone.

The crowd erupted into an outcry of shock. Storey grimaced as she looked at it. That hand was beyond creepy. "I don't know if it matters or not, but I don't remember much about drawing that picture."

Eric's father groaned and smacked his hand down on the table. "That just makes it worse. How could you?"

"How could I what? Draw? I've always drawn. It's never created portals into another dimension. Keep in mind, I wouldn't have done anything if you people hadn't left that instrument behind on your invasion."

"Invasion? Did she just say invasion?"

"What invasion? What is she talking about?"

Paxton once again held up his hand to bring the conversation back under control. "We're not pointing fingers here. A series of accidents has brought us to this spot. We have to focus. We are in a crisis, let's deal with that."

Arguments and shouting broke out across the room. Storey slunk low in her chair. Who could get used to all this fighting?

"Stop," roared Paxton. "We have to find out what this drawing represents. And if it is what I think it is, we have to find a solution – fast."

Eric's father shot a disgusted look at Storey. "This is just a drawing. She can't possibly wield the power of the stylus."

Another elder seated at the table spoke up. "Just what are you thinking the problem is here?"

Paxton addressed the room, his voice deep and deadly serious. "I'm afraid it's the Louers."

Dead silence. Then absolute chaos erupted.

Louers? Storey wracked her brain. Nope, the name meant nothing to her. Obviously, it did to everyone else as questions flew at Paxton too fast for him to answer.

"The Louers. Oh my. I thought they'd been wiped out."

"Are they real?"

"We got rid of them, didn't we?"

The questions rose and fell all around her. As she caught the gist of the conversation, the puzzle pieces fell into place. Storey thought she finally understood. "Are you saying this hand belongs to one of those Louers? And that by drawing a doorway, I actually created a door they could open too?"

"Exactly." Paxton nodded like she was some favorite student. She'd love to be, except her next question would drop her right down to a failing grade.

"So who and what are the Louers?"

CHAPTER 8

HER HISTORY LESSON wouldn't start until later. By that time, Storey expected to be comatose. It didn't seem to matter which side of the veil she was on. Neither side could get an agreement out of a group of people – decision by committee was a waste of time. The bickering had been going on for hours. At least it felt that way to Storey.

"We should set up a committee to study the problem. We'll appoint an overseer who can pick his team and set out steps as to how to proceed."

"Oh, not this again." Storey groaned as the same idea was hashed over and over again.

"What?" asked a skinny, bald-headed guy dressed similarly to Paxton. "Have you got a better idea?"

"Hell, yes." The same hush fell over the room as she once again lost her cool. "Oh, right, I swore again. Well, I've got to tell you – it's a little hard to have any respect for a group of people who are so busy trying to get someone else to make a decision that nothing gets done." She stood up, ignoring Eric's restraining hand on her forearm. "I know I don't understand how things work over here, but maybe someone could answer a couple of questions. Such as, can I draw the door closed? Can I rip up the paper and have it no longer exist? How about I draw a group of people taking these Louers and forcing them back to the other side?"

"Will someone shut this girl up. She's wasting our time and has caused us nothing but trouble. Someone get her out of here." Eric's father, the arrogant asshole, appeared to be some kind of leader here.

"Why? Because I'm trying to understand what we can and can't do. It seems logical that if the stylus opened the door, it could close it, too." She strove to keep her voice reasonable.

"I don't think it works like that," Eric whispered.

"That's the problem. None of you know how this works." She spread her hands out on the table. "You're all so used to doing something one way that you can't see there might be another way to approach the problem."

"It's not that. There are rules on our side. The Louers were our enemies. Since they've been gone we've had peace."

"Yeah? Did you go on secret research missions and steal from them, too?" she scoffed. "You guys need to work on your communication skills."

"And you need to stop insulting us."

"Why?" she challenged. "What are you going to do?" She stood, reached across the table for her sketchbook, and then walked to the doorway. "You don't want me here. I'm obviously of no value, so pardon me if I leave." She strode out, letting her sarcasm fill the room.

"Don't let her leave. Eric, stop her," the Councilman shouted.

Eric stood up and snorted as Storey walked away. "What do you want me to do?"

"Well, she can't just run loose over here. Who knows what kind of damage she could cause?"

Eric snorted again. "Like we do in her world. It's not like we registered with her any of her governments and sign in and out on our visits. Neither are we under guard at any time."

The Councilman's icy voice sliced through the room. "Lock her up. She's the enemy."

Storey gasped and spun around. Seeing the vindictive look on his fat face, she headed for the doorway.

"No, wait." Eric raced behind her.

His father called back. "Eric. She's not one of us. Remember your place."

Shooting his father a disgusted look, Eric left the conference room. He caught up with her in the lab. "What are you doing?"

"Going home. I came here at your request. I can't help you. Therefore, I'm going home."

"You can't just leave. Don't you understand? This is a different dimension. You can't just walk home." Eric ran his hand through his hair. "I know this is tough, and I'm sorry. I'd forgotten what it's like when this group gets together.

"It's called bureaucracy on my side."

"Yeah. Same thing here."

"And yes, I can just leave." Storey waved the stylus and sketchbook at him.

"What, you're just going to draw the other side? And expect to walk right into it?"

"Or something that's even easier." She sat down cross-legged on the floor and sketched madly for a couple of minutes while Eric watched over her shoulder.

"There's no way that's going to work," he scoffed.

"Maybe and maybe not," she answered him without raising her gaze from her picture. "Then again, you're so used to the rules of your world that you don't even know if the rules can be broken. And sometimes you don't need to break anything. You need to find a way around things."

He squatted down beside her. "True. I'd think you might need to know the rules before you can break them."

"Apparently not or we wouldn't be in this mess now." She shot him a grin before refocusing. "Wait and see. If it doesn't work, no problem, then you can use your decoder and take me home." She finished her drawing, painfully aware of his lack of response. She stood up and waited until he'd straightened and looked at her. "They won't let you take me home, will they?"

He grimaced, dropping his gaze to the ground and kicked out as if at an invisible rock. "No."

"Well, you're going to have to if this doesn't work," she said coolly. "You brought me here, so it's up to you to do the right thing and take me home. Especially as you brought me here without my permission in the first place. You said you wanted to show someone my work. You didn't say I'd be going to another dimension to make that happen. And you didn't say I wouldn't be going home."

"Let's hope this works, so I'm not put into that position."

Studying her sketch, Storey added, "Seems like parental control, discrimination and assholes are all the same no matter which side of the veil you're on. Too bad. I was hoping your society was more advanced and my people could learn something from you. Not going to happen, though."

"We *are* more advanced," he protested.

She walked over to the wall she'd been staring at. Nodding once, she ripped off the paper and looked around. "Do you oh-so-much-more-superior people have such things as pins or tape?"

He snorted, walked over to the closest bench and pulled

off a piece of something gray. Returning to her side, he said, "It's neither and won't cause any damage like those two will."

She sniffed disdainfully. "We have sticky stuff like that at home too." Flipping her hair, she stuck the gray ball onto the back of the sketch and hung it on the wall. Taking a few steps back, she studied the picture in relationship to the rest of the room, grabbed her pencil and drew a couple of quick horizontal and then vertical lines on the wall outside of the picture. She nodded. "Okay. See you around – maybe."

She walked purposefully toward the picture that she'd incorporated the wall into.

"Eric, what are you two doing?" Paxton ran into the room. "We need you back in there. Bring Storey so we can keep track of her."

Storey shook her head. Not going to happen. She was going home. With a small wave of her fingers, she walked into the wall – and through her picture.

"No. Oh, no. She can't do—"

Storey grinned as she stood in the middle of her own bedroom.

Apparently, she could.

ERIC'S JAW DROPPED.

Paxton stood in place, wringing his hands. "Oh dear. Not good. This is not good."

Eric blinked, then blinked again. She'd done it. Even after he'd said she couldn't. How stupid could he be? And not just him. His people were just as guilty. She'd been right. They'd been locked into the surety of knowing what worked and what didn't. Therefore, they'd never questioned the boundaries of that knowledge.

Storey hadn't had the same restrictions. She'd taken the steps to find out just what she could do.

Unbelievable. Shocking really. He pulled himself out of the dangerous bout of admiration to study the doorway Storey had opened, then backed up several feet. She'd drawn a hallway, as if the picture on the wall was a portion of the wall itself. Using the doorway to her bedroom as the vanishing point in the distance, she'd created a long hallway to her room. A perspective drawing with her room as the single point in the center.

Brilliant, really.

Eric turned to face his mentor and received another shock.

Paxton was terrified.

He'd never thought to see fear on Paxton's face. Consternation, even worry, anger, but fear, now that was a new one. One he didn't like.

"Oh, dear. What are we going to do?" Paxton held his hands together and stared at the wall.

"What's going on here? Where's the girl?" His father bellowed from the doorway.

Eric stiffened. Maybe it was Storey's influence, or maybe, he was just seeing the light for the first time. He pulled the sketch off the wall and folded it.

"The girl? *Storey* has gone home."

Eric braced for the storm to hit.

"What? You took her home? How dare you? You will be punished for this."

Years of being educated in a strict school, where obedience and respect for his father, their leader, was all that held Eric back from letting the words spill over. He could only stare in disgust at his father, a father who'd been absent from most of his life. "I didn't take her back."

"Not directly, but you let her leave," Paxton cried out in anguish. "Oh, dear. This is terrible."

"She was never a prisoner, Paxton. She came at my request. To show you her picture. Realizing that no one here would listen to her or wanted her help, she decided to go home."

"She was supposed to have been your prisoner. It's your fault," snapped his father.

"Why? I was told to retrieve the stylus. Nothing about trying to keep Story captive. Not that I could have," he added thoughtfully, staring at the wall.

"You could have used chains and the dungeon. At least they'd have gotten the job done."

Cold settled into Eric's chest. The dungeons were for the worst of the worst. Dark, wet and miles underground where prisoners went insane or, more often than not, died of neglect. Originally built for a different purpose, the only prisoners ever sent there were traitors. People who went against the Council. If they'd planned that for Storey, he was glad she'd escaped. Since when had his people been so harsh, so unforgiving? Being on the inside, he'd never questioned his way of life or those in power. No one did. Everyone had what they needed. At least as far as he knew. Why worry? For the first time in his life he questioned the morality of his government. "Our dungeons have never been for anyone but slaves, when we had them, and the worst criminals in our society. There's so few of them the dungeons aren't worth maintaining. I hardly think Storey's actions warrant such a punishment."

"Well, possibly not the dungeons." His father backed

down on that point. "But we can't just have her running around loose on the other side. Who knows who'd she'll tell? What damage she'll do?"

Eric shook his head in disbelief. "She's just a kid."

"She's already caused damage." Paxton came to Eric, as if willing him to understand. "You have to see the truth here. She can't be left to do as she pleases."

Eric cocked his head, fear for Storey and a deep-seated anger slowly building, twisting into a fury he'd never known. "What is it you're planning to do?"

"You must bring her back, of course. Even a dimwit like you should be able to see the sense of that." The sneer on his father's face sharpened.

The fury boiling behind his self control was going to kill him. He swallowed hard. "Really. *I'm* to bring her back so she can be your prisoner? So you can take away her memories, force her to be a lab rat for you to study?"

Paxton suddenly rose to his full height. "Don't use that tone with me. Of course she must come back. She still has the stylus."

"Which is soulbound to her. They can't be separated anymore."

"We don't know that. Sarcov has almost recovered. He might be able to bond with it again."

"It can only bond with one person at a time."

"Right. So now you see how important it is to get it back," his father snapped.

Eric stared at the two men, his anger being quietly drowned by fear. "You can't take it away from her unless she dies or, as in Sarcov's case, it appears as if death is imminent. Storey is neither of those."

"Oh, don't be naive. She's dangerous. Of course, she's

going to have to die – eventually.”

No. No, surely that’s not what he was hearing. Eric shook his head slowly like a bull with a red flag being waved in his face. “You want me to bring her back so you can kill her?”

“Well, I wouldn’t put it that way.” Paxton tried to smooth the harshness of the conversation over. “We might need her.”

“Her name is Storey. The least you can do is call her by her proper name.”

“What are you talking about? She’s one of them.” His father’s outrage boiled over. “They don’t deserve our respect. They’re animals. Mindless in their actions, eating and killing their way through life with no consequence for their future.”

Eric reared back. “And what’s so different about what you’re suggesting? Didn’t you just tell me to go and get her, so you could kill her?” He sneered. “How dare you put yourself on a pedestal above her and her kind? Is this what you’ve raised me for? To view myself as better than the others just because they live on the other side of the veil?”

“We are more advanced than they are. Our technology is superior, so are our energy capabilities. We must protect our way of life.” Paxton tried to appease him. “These humans would overrun us with sheer numbers, strip us of our knowledge, our resources. You can see that, right?”

“We don’t have any information on what they can or cannot do. Storey said something else that’s true. We’ve gone over to her world time and time again, bringing back anything we wanted or needed to develop our technology. That’s the *only* reason we’ve developed beyond them. We’ve never once shared what we’ve learned, including the new medicines and healing lasers that have wiped out illness here.

No. She's right – we've stolen everything from them."

"Nonsense. We're doing what we've always done. We've lived like this for centuries. How can you start to judge our ways now? That girl is dangerous. Look at how you are speaking to me. You've never talked back before." His father snorted at him.

Eric frowned at the truth of his father's words. When his father had said to do something, he'd done it – blindly. Regardless of right or wrong. There'd been a time or two when he'd wondered at the wisdom of the orders, but had followed them regardless.

How horrible was that? Shame filled him for his past actions, or lack thereof, and for his own treatment of Storey. She deserved better. He'd tricked her into coming over here and hadn't even taken her home again.

"Now, I want you to go there and bring her back." His father drew himself up to his full height which, being more than a foot shorter than Paxton at his side, made him look ridiculous. "And I want you to go now."

Eric tilted his head and studied him. Paxton waited, holding his breath. Eric ignored him. "And if I don't? Then what?"

His father's face turned beet red and absolute rage shone from his eyes. He gritted his teeth and stuck his jaw out. "What did you say to me?"

"I asked you what the penalty would be if I refuse to commit murder." Eric raised his eyebrows. "That is what you are asking of me, isn't it? If I bring her back, you will kill her. That makes me an accomplice in the eyes of the law."

"No. I am not going to argue about this. This person, this girl, has threatened national security. She doesn't get a trial and there won't be any charge of murder. She is a danger to us all."

"Says you."

His father went seriously quiet. When he spoke again, his voice was flat and dark. "I am going to make myself clear right now and we will never speak of this again." Steel shone from his eyes. "I am ordering you to go to the other side of the veil, retrieve the girl, and bring her back here. Should you fail to do so, you are guilty of the same crime of which she is accused. And then…" he paused for effect, "a team will go over there and do what you weren't willing to do your-self – by force if necessary."

Paxton closed his eyes and bowed his head as if the worst had happened.

A chill swept over Eric. This was his father. The father he'd idolized growing up. The father he'd respected all through his brief years. The father he'd done everything to impress was ordering him to bring Storey back to be killed – or be killed himself.

"STOREY? IS THAT you?" Her mother burst into her bed-room. "There you are. I swear I seem to spend half my time looking for you lately."

"I'm here, Mom. What's up?" Storey hated the coolness in her own tone. Her day hadn't been the best to begin with. She warmed her smile.

"Oh, Eric didn't come back with you, did he?" Her mother peered around the corner of her room as if looking for signs of him hidden in the closet.

"No, Mom. He had to go home."

"Oh." She smiled brightly. "He seems like such a nice boy."

"Yes, he seems nice." Then, looks could be deceiving, as she'd found out.

"Is he…special?" Her mother's hopeful expression fell as Storey shook her head. "You two looked so great together."

"Maybe. Unlikely. I don't know. I wouldn't get my hopes up, if I were you." Storey knew her Mom had watched her social life with a wary eye during her relationship with Jeff and immediately afterwards.

"Well, if it's meant to be and all that." She smiled. "Why don't you come down and have a cup of tea with me?"

"Who's here?"

The smile dropped from her mom's face fast. She hesitated. "Do you resent all the company? I never thought." She nibbled on her bottom lip. "We do have a lot of company though, don't we? I'm sorry. It's your home, too."

Oh, brother. "Mom. Stop. I'm fine with the company. I'm glad you have so many friends. That you're happy with your life and your beliefs." Mostly, anyways, but she wasn't going to open up that discussion. Not now.

A smile peeped out. "I wish you'd consider joining…"

"I know. At the moment, I'm not feeling it." Although after what she'd seen today, Wiccan didn't seem as odd or farfetched as it had yesterday. "I'll make my own decision. I just need some time."

"Then time you shall have." She smiled. "And there's no one downstairs right now. Let's go have a cup of tea and some fresh poppy seed cake."

"Best offer I've had all day." In a rare moment of concord, the two linked arms and headed for the kitchen.

Storey could only hope her bedroom would still be empty when she returned. She'd forgotten to consider one tiny problem – how to close the portal she'd created from her side.

CHAPTER 9

GETTING ALONG WITH your mother beat trying to avoid her. Two hours later, Storey headed to her bedroom door, yawning. She had homework to finish but no energy to care about such minor details. Pushing her door open, she came to a sudden halt.

She gasped, checked behind her to make sure she was alone before stepping in a shutting the door behind her. "Oh my God," she hissed. "What are you doing here?" Leaning against the door, she stared at Eric, who lay half asleep on her bed. Damn, he looked good there. As if he belonged.

Not.

"About time you got here. I've been waiting forever."

"Why? What do you want from me?" Pulling out her computer chair, she sat down facing him, before her knees gave out on her. "And how did you get in?"

"Same way you did, only I removed the paper as I went through so we couldn't be followed."

She raised an eyebrow. "Cool. Too bad I didn't think of that. Then again, I wasn't sure if it would work in the first place."

"Well, it's not there anymore."

"Thank God. It's a little creepy to have people entering my bedroom from another dimension. Maybe the kitchen or living room, but not my bedroom, thanks."

He just stared at her.

"Okay, I'm babbling. Sorry. It's just a little unnerving to have you here out of the blue like that." She stared out the window.

"They want me to bring you back."

She tilted her head and studied the look on his face. Odd wording. Hmmm. "And what do you want to do?"

"I don't want you to go over there again."

She raised an eyebrow. So much for seeing where the relationship with Eric might go. Long distance didn't quite cut it, as she already knew. Look what had happened to her and Jeff.

"Good, then I won't. The last visit was enough for me, anyway."

"They'll send someone else if I don't bring you back."

The shadows lengthened in the early evening light. "They again." She watched him carefully, sensing more to the story. "How much force will 'they' use to make me go back?"

His face paled.

Her stomach twisted. "That much, huh?" She didn't want to dwell on it. They didn't look like the kind of group that lived and let live. "Did they come to an agreement about the Louers yet?"

Eric shook his head. "I think they're more concerned about you being a loose end."

Her eyes widened. "They're afraid of me? Of what I might say? Do?" At each successive nod, the knots in her stomach tightened. She closed her eyes. Think, damn it. There had to be a way out of this mess. "What are my options?"

"I don't know. I've been lying here and going over them.

None are great."

"List those you've considered."

He appeared to choose his words carefully as he listed off choices that included him never going back, going back and helping his people after negotiating her return, hiding by moving to another part of the planet so the people coming behind him wouldn't be able to find her.

As he rambled on, she had a distinct sense that something was wrong. "Okay, out with it. Something else happened. What?"

He sat up and swung his feet over the bed. "They'll kill you if you go back."

She swallowed. Hard. "As a conversationalist, you suck."

His lopsided grin slipped out. "Sorry. Not used to this kind of conversation."

The grin did it, easing the weight on her chest threatening to suffocate her. She grinned back. "Yeah, it shows. So they don't want to leave any witnesses behind, huh?"

"Something like that."

Silence fell.

"You're serious, aren't you?" How had everything gone so wrong? A few days ago life had been normal. She'd been wishing for something new and different to come into her life. A death squad from another dimension wasn't what she'd had in mind. "So, if I go with you they will kill me. If I don't go with you they'll send a team over to retrieve me then kill me anyway? Where's the option that lets me live?"

"I think that's the run part, so they can't find you."

"Except you have technology that allows your people to track me, while I don't have anything to help me evade your people. So that's hardly an option." She studied the fatigue in his eyes. He looked like he'd been to hell and back. "What happens to you if I don't go back with you? Anything? Or just a slap on the wrist because you didn't follow orders?"

He stood up straight, his face lean and ravaged. "Death. The Council says I will face a death sentence if you don't go back with me."

Storey couldn't believe it. Studying his face in disbelief, she found the truth in his pain. Eric's father was head of the Council. If he'd ordered his son's death over this…he was a monster. "Why would your father do that?"

"According to him, you're a threat to national security and that outweighs his parental concern."

"Bullshit."

He winced.

She laughed bitterly. "Sorry, but that's a load of crap. There's no way I'm a security issue. He's power tripping."

"Maybe, but it's effective. He issued the order in front of witnesses. It has to be carried out. There is no rescinding that kind of order."

She stood and stared up at his face. Nothing like parents to remind you of your humanity. "I'm sorry. It has to hurt to hear your life has so little value."

He snorted. "You think?"

"I'm not going back there. Not so they can use me as a lab rat and then kill me out of their own fear."

His eyes stared down at her, closed briefly then opened, bright blue lights shining deep. "I know and I wouldn't want you to."

"Except that means your death."

"I know," he said, his face seriously grim, his decision clearly made.

She respected him in that moment.

"Okay, this is ridiculous. Now that we've settled that,

let's come up with a way to make this right for both of us."

"Do you think that's possible?"

It was that faint hope peering from deep inside his eyes that settled her determination to find a solution. One where they both got to live.

ERIC STOMPED ON the hope trickling through him. It wouldn't do to put too much credence in Storey's skills. What she'd achieved so far was phenomenal. But he had to face reality. Paxton hadn't helped after his father had stormed off. "You shouldn't have pushed him like that."

"I pushed him?" Astonished, Eric could only stare at his beloved mentor.

"Yes, you forced him to declare his intentions with the girl. He can't back down now. We might have found a way around this mess but for that."

"Like what?" he scoffed. "She's right, you know. We're all about us. Not about them. Everything is our way. The mistake was ours in the first place."

"She didn't have to pick up the stylus," Paxton said fretfully.

"She hardly had a choice – it called to her. You said yourself that it wanted to go home. No one is looking at that. People need to realize she's a victim here. The stylus targeted *her*. She didn't mean to do this. She had no idea that she could do any of this."

"Regardless of how this started, she's in the middle of it now. We have no solution to the Louers either."

"She'd have been happy to help."

Paxton snuck a glance around the room, then leaned forward to whisper, "Do you think so?" At Eric's nod, he said, "Then go bring her back. Please. Our very existence is at stake here."

Eric studied the older man. Did he believe that? Or was it just another attempt to get Eric to do his bidding? "I can't deliver her to her death."

"Don't think of it that way. It would be a state sentence being carried out."

"It's murder." Eric said. "I'd be bringing her back under false pretences."

"No. Not at all. Tell her we need her help."

"And what?" Eric threw up his hands. "And don't tell her that as thanks, we're going to brand her as a traitor to the state and have her killed? Are you insane?"

Paxton reared back. "No. But if you don't bring her back, then a retrieval team will go after her anyway and you'll both be killed."

Eric had contemplated the two horrible options. He didn't want to die. Neither could he let Storey be killed. "Even when the orders are wrong?" Fatigue slid through his voice. He was more tired than he could believe, and none of it was related to how he felt physically. The emotional stress of the last few hours had leeched everything from his system.

He glanced around the lab where he'd enjoyed so many comfortable hours with Paxton. Paxton had been more of a father to him than his own flesh and blood version. "Tell me, would you bring her back, knowing you were bringing her to her death?"

"If I had to, as much as I don't like the idea, yes."

"Why is it a 'had to?' Why is death the only option? She's not going to hurt us – particularly once she understands the problem."

"You don't know that. We have to get the stylus back.

That she should be bound to it is intolerable."

"Why? Maybe they have soulbound objects over there."

"We've seen no sign of such a thing."

"Again that arrogance. We haven't seen them, therefore, they don't exist? Why do you insist we're better than they are?"

"That's not what I said. Don't go putting words in my mouth." Paxton's voice turned testy. "Get ready. It shouldn't take you long to find her."

"It won't be easy to persuade her to return," warned Eric. Already he was calculating how long they had to make their getaway.

"Don't take too long. Your father will give you a few hours, overnight probably. If you're not back by noon tomorrow, a retrieval team will be sent over."

"Is anyone else over there now?"

"No. There aren't any planned missions in the next year."

"Hmmm. Just wondered if we had spies living on the other side of the veil."

Paxton stared at him in shock. "Of course not. We've never done that. What for? They've never been a threat to us before."

"And they still aren't."

"It's time for you to do what you need to do." Paxton gave him a hard look.

Eric frowned, studying Paxton's face. Had there been a weird inflection in Paxton's voice? The wording had been interesting. *Do what you need to do.*

Now, lying here in Storey's room, that's the phrase he focused on.

"Hey, are you there? Felt like I lost you somewhere, just

now."

"I'm here."

He stared at her, his gaze flat and concerned, for a long moment. Long enough for her sunny smile to fall away and be replaced by a worried frown.

"Run away with me."

"WHAT DID YOU say?" she squeaked. Was that horrible, high-pitched girlie voice really hers? *Oh God.*

"It's the only option. I can teach you how to evade my people, and you can teach me to live over here."

"Why run, then?" she asked cautiously.

He stared at her again in that deep, intense way, as if he could see to the center of her soul. Maybe he could. His people seemed to have untold skills and technology, she thought resentfully.

"The retrieval team won't be polite. I'm afraid of the lengths they might go to get the information they want from your family."

"Oh my God. Are you saying they might hurt my mother?" At his slow nod, she collapsed beside him on the bed. "This is so not happening. I didn't care until you mentioned my mom getting hurt." She buried her face in her hands. "I've been so stupid."

A warm hand squeezed her shoulder. She dropped her hands to find him leaning over her.

"You haven't been stupid. That you managed to do what you did, took a remarkable amount of resourcefulness and ingenuity."

"Really?" She raised an eyebrow at him, inordinately pleased when he nodded. So he thought she was smart. Well good. She was no dummy. She knew that. "Running away isn't the answer."

"Why not?" He sat down beside her and held her hand. "We can't fight. There are too many of them."

"Maybe. Once we start there'll be no end to our running. No, we have to find a way to remove the 'kill order' from my head."

"My father won't back down. He believes you're a threat and that's that."

She studied his face. "For a society that talks and doesn't act, it seems odd that he'd make one statement and then stand by it."

"That's why they talk so much first. Once they embark on a course of action, they stand by it."

"What if we kidnap him – until he changes his mind?" Eric looked so horrified, she had to laugh. "Kidding! But we need to do something offensive instead of defensive. Once you're on the defensive, it's hard to get off of it."

"What, did you take Spy 101?"

Tossing her hair over her shoulder, she grinned. "Football."

His shock had her laughing out loud.

"Then we kidnap someone other than my father. The security surrounding him is impressive."

"What about your security?" she asked curiously. Did no one care about Eric?

"Don't have any."

Nice father, worried more about protecting himself than his son, but she refrained from pointing that out. "Could we negotiate?"

He frowned. "I don't understand."

"What if I offer to help, providing the death sentence is

rescinded?" she chewed her bottom lip, worried by one big issue. "And can we trust them to keep their part of the agreement afterward?" She wasn't sure they could. "Hmmm. Why are the Louers so feared?"

"It has to do with the kind of people they are. They're more like a pestilence that feeds on others. Literally."

"Gross. Are you saying they're cannibals?"

"Supposedly. At least according to the archives they're human-like, but more animal in behavior."

"Like a dog? Horse? A monkey kind of thing?" She couldn't quite reconcile the long boney fingers pushing the door open in her drawing with any kind of animal.

"I don't know."

"Or are they just 'lesser people' like your kind consider me to be?"

"I'm not sure." He frowned. "I hope not. Everything I've learned has come from the archives."

"Written by your unbiased ancestors, no doubt." Storey snickered. "Why were they locked away in this third dimension anyway? And don't forget that outside of that hand in my drawing, there's been no sign of Louers in either dimension."

"As far as the archives report," he admitted at her knowing look, "they hunted my people. They had stealth and skills that gave them the upper hand in wars. We were a peaceful people. They made us slaves. It's said that they ate our kind, as well."

"Well, the slave thing certainly isn't new and neither is the war. Your people were the weaker of the two and lost the fight. Maybe your people did something to bring the battle on their heads, and they rose up against you."

His gaze widened. "No."

Storey wasn't so sure. It might have happened that way. If Eric's people were in any way like her own, war was almost second nature. And Eric might not know all the facts. After seeing his people in action, she doubted they were as innocent as he'd like to believe. His wouldn't be the first society to wipe their history, and therefore their record, clean. She'd learned that much in history class. "How long do we have?"

"Until early tomorrow, I'd say."

"Does Paxton monitor all the screens all the time?"

"Yes. He or someone on his staff."

"Then why don't we go back to your world? They can see that you did your job and…" she held up her hand to forestall his words from flying out, "and then you can help me escape again."

He rose and stormed around the small room. "Because I can't guarantee your safety."

She nodded. "That's why we're going to have to be crafty."

"I don't understand."

"Come on, I'll show you." She snatched up her sketch-book and sat down beside him.

"Storey, are you in there?" Her mother knocked on her door. Panic-stricken, Storey turned to face the door as Eric tried to squeeze his length into her closet, scrunching beneath her hanging clothes. Grabbing her mp3 player, Storey walked to the door and opened it, a quizzical smile on her face. "Of course I am. What's up?" Music blasted from the cheap earbud in her hand, the other one sat in her ear.

"I thought I heard you talking to someone."

Storey snorted. "Yeah, right. As if. I don't have anyone to talk to, remember?"

"Well, Eric would talk to you. He seemed like such nice boy."

Uh oh. She so didn't want her mother talking about this, especially not when Eric could hear. She shook her head. "We're not going there, Mom."

"I just wanted to tell you I'm heading over to Sandra and Daren's place, if you don't mind, that is?" She appeared anxious, as if waiting for Storey's approval.

Storey sighed. "Mom, that's great. Go have fun. No, I don't want to join you, and yes, it's totally fine that you're going."

Her mom gave her a worried look. "Are you sure?"

Maybe it was the imminent threat of death or the thought of her mom waking up to find her gone – maybe forever – that prompted Storey. Regardless, she leaned forward and kissed her mom on the cheek. "I'm sure. Go have fun."

Relieved, her mom turned away. "There's some snack food downstairs if you get hungry later."

"We just ate, Mom. I'm fine."

"You didn't eat much. I could…"

"No. You couldn't. Stop. I'm old enough to know when I need to eat. I'm not hungry. If that changes, I promise I'll go and find something."

"Okay then. I might be late, so I'll see you in the morning."

"G'night, Mom."

Storey closed the door and turned to lean against it with a heavy sigh. Her mother would be devastated if something happened to her only child.

"You okay?"

"Yeah. Let's get started." Story crossed over to the bed

and opened her sketchbook to a clean page. "Where are they likely to take me, once we get to your side?"

"The worst case would be the dungeons."

She gave him a horrified look. "What? That sounds bad."

"It is. Nasty place. Most prisoners sicken and die." He pondered the idea. "I don't think they would start with that punishment."

"Good," she muttered. "I'm looking to draw exits from your world to mine."

"That's risky," he warned. "I can't guarantee where they might take you."

"True. However, if you hand me over and I have some exits on me already, then I could get home if I don't happen to care for the accommodations. And I need to take spare paper for my stylus, just in case."

He shook his head. "You're going to have to be so care-ful. If they catch you, they'll take the stylus away from you and you won't be able to use it."

"This is why I want to draw the exits now. While I have the stylus." She twisted the pencil in her hand. "Do you think I could draw a weapon? An assistant? A new happy world for your people? Like what are the limits of this thing?" She stared down at the pencil, wondering just what was possible. "Have you used one yourself?"

"No. There are very few of them in existence, and they bond to the death, so a new bonding can only happen when the owner dies."

"And mine belonged to a scientist? Weird." She studied the pencil, trying to read the writing trying to not think about what might happen to her if the Torans took it back. "So no one really knows what they can do."

"No."

"If I draw a cupcake with it, will it create one?"

"I don't think so. Whatever you draw has to be contained in the paper."

Scrunching up her face, she struggled with what he was saying. "So I drew a door and the paper became the door. If I draw a window and hold it up, can I see what's on the other side?"

Confusion filled his gaze and then he blinked hard. "It's not like the picture is going to change and show you what's there. Maybe you can put your face through the paper or something. I don't know. Honestly, I think you're going to have to try it out."

"Except I don't want a window unless I could see something useful. Like into the dungeon so I could see the walls and then draw them as a way to create a door out again."

"Hmm. Not going to work."

A weird sound rumbled through her room. She bolted upright. "What the hell is that?"

Eric got his feet more slowly. "I'm not sure. It can't be good."

The noise sounded again, under her feet. She bolted upright. "I'm going to look."

With Eric on her heels, she raced downstairs to the living room. Her mother had gone, leaving the house empty. She dashed into the den, which sat right below her bedroom. The far wall had splintered and cracked. As they stood and watched, several strangely long, bony fingers crept through the crack, breaking pieces of plaster as they slid further out. Dirty and rough, with short, cracked fingernails, the fingers scrabbled for a hold on the wall.

"Oh shit. Oh shit."

Eric gulped audibly. Running his hand through his hair, he stared at those fingers in horror. A quick glance at his face confirmed Storey's suspicions.

"The Louers?" she whispered in dread. At his nod, her heart pounded inside her chest and her mind screamed at her. How could this have happened? Why were they *here* and not on Eric's side? She'd never considered this. She looked around for something, anything, to make this all go away. She glanced down at her hand, still holding the sketchbook and stylus.

Crouching down, she balanced the book on her knee and slapped down a sketch of the wall in front of her, without the crack. Then she added a door and placed a deadbolt on the side, separating the two worlds. She could have done it in half the time, but her fingers were trembling so badly, she kept messing up.

With one clean stroke of the stylus, she locked the deadbolt in place. And sat back to stare up at wall, her chest heaving from the effort. Her breath caught in her throat. Did it work?

No. Maybe? The hand was still there. It tried to wiggle as if struggling to move but incapable.

Eric gasped.

"Oh shit," She sketched faster, drawing in the crack to resemble, as close as possible, the damage to the wall in front of her. There was a hard snap, and the fingers disappeared. Then she drew a paint brush in the act of painting the entire wall in plaster. Her breath labored as she struggled to keep her panic under control.

Using a stick hand, she quickly sketched the brush moving across the wall covering up the hand and the crack. As soon as she finished, she looked over the top of the book.

The hand was gone and the cracks in her wall were gone – at least where the paint brush had stroked. On a hunch, she turned to a clean page and drew another paint brush, wrote 'eraser' on it then ripped it crudely off the page. With Eric watching her in astonishment, she folded the paper such that only the brush shape showed. Walking to the damaged wall, she stroked, erasing the mess there. Unbelievably, one stroke at a time, everything disappeared. Panicked still, she couldn't stop until the last of it was gone and the wall looked as it had before. Even then, her hand continued to rub the eraser over the wall.

Eric grabbed her hand and pulled her gently into his arms. "It's done, stop!"

Shuddering, she gasped for breath. "Oh, my God."

"You can say that again."

"So much for not being able to create tools."

Holding her tight, he rested his chin on her head. "I can't believe you just did that."

"I didn't do anything. It was the stylus." She took a deep shuddering breath and let it out. "Do you think they're gone?" Pulling back, she peered up at him. "Like really gone?"

"I don't know. What about the outside of the house? Did that fix the problem or just hide this side?"

She shot him a horrified glance and bolted toward the front door. The screen door banged behind her as she ran outside and around to the back of the house. Eric raced around the corner as she was backing up to take a wider look. There were no cracks, no broken siding. Nothing to say anything odd had occurred at all.

Her breath gusted out. Hands on hips, she surveyed the back wall in amazement. "That thing was coming through the wall – as in *between* the inside and outside walls."

"No." Eric reached out a hand to touch the wooden siding. "That's the part that still confuses you. He was coming between the dimensions. Good thing it was the living room. He could have just as easily come through your bedroom." He glanced at her. "I gotta tell you, that was incredibly quick thinking on your part."

She flushed, grateful for the darkness, and wiped her hands on her jeans. "Thanks. I didn't think at all about it. I just reacted."

The evening air was cool. She shivered as she walked back around to the front of her house. "I wonder if it was the stylus telling me what to do?" His quick frown had her adding, "Or don't you think it can communicate?"

They walked up the three steps to the front porch and Eric opened the door for her. "You tell me. By now you know more than I do. Keep in mind the stylus probably doesn't know or care about the Louers. It seems to just want to get home."

Still the idea had come at the right time, and she couldn't help wonder at the intelligence level of the stylus. She studied it as she had so many times already. It looked like a thick art pencil. Remarkably unremarkable. And it was anything but.

Back inside, she returned to the once damaged wall, looking for proof of the event. Her fingers tentatively stroked the painted drywall. Sure enough, a tiny spider network of cracks dotted the wall and left the paint cracking. It didn't look bad, just old and unloved. She rubbed her temple. "Wonder how long before my mother notices."

"Hopefully forever."

Storey snorted. "Oh, she'll see it. All of a sudden she's

going to realize how weary and old the room looks and will want to repaint."

Now that the crisis had passed, she had to admit she felt a little shaky. Or maybe shocky was a better word.

"I think we should leave."

"Yeah? Your world or mine?" She studied the worry etched in his wrinkled forehead.

"It's possible the Louers made it into my world." The frown rippled across his features. "If they did, my people are particularly vulnerable to them."

Storey glanced back at the wall. "In what way?"

"They're terrified of them, for one. We were raised knowing our people were once enslaved until they couldn't work anymore and ended up as food. Plus, my people aren't fighters. We don't have wars."

"Ever? Amazing. Kinda cool, too. Who'd have thought an entire species of people could survive without trying to kill each other off?" She searched his face wondering if he was telling the truth. Or the truth as he understood it.

"Never," he said firmly.

"Only with the Louers?"

"Yes."

"Not even with my people?"

"No. We fell across your world in our attempt to banish the Louers."

"So then there could be many other dimensions out there?"

He paused, as if considering this for the first time. "I don't know that there aren't. We've never come across any, though."

"And you've never gone looking." Interesting. As long as something didn't cross their path they didn't go out of their way to learn more. Not a curious people. But rigid, in keeping to what they knew. Not liking change, or progress, or criticism, apparently. Good to know. Could she turn their traits against them in her bid for freedom?

CHAPTER 10

"ARE YOU SURE you want to do this?"

Straightening up, Storey winced at her backache. She'd collapsed to the floor an hour ago when they'd finally retreated to her bedroom from the family room. Her last drawing was finished. She stared at the stack for a long moment. There were a million events she couldn't plan for. A thousand more she might not be able to handle. There was no way to plan for every contingency.

For what had to be the twelfth time, Storey nodded at him as she slouched onto her bed. There was no point in trying to get Eric on board with the plan. He belonged to a society of talkers. She couldn't expect more than that from him. A teeny bit of her was disappointed. She could have used an action man right now. Sex appeal was great, but could she count on Eric when things went wrong?

She didn't know. She could only hope so. Someone needed to watch her back.

She wanted, no needed, to have paper and the stylus with her at all times. She wondered if there was a way to duplicate or split the stylus. To have two, a dummy one they might believe was real and confiscate so she could keep hers. In fact, she probably had something similar in her art kit. And that was something worth checking out. How would they know?

Scrunching up her face, she considered the problem of duplicating the stylus. There was only one way to find out. She picked up the pencil and drew a picture of it on the page in front of her. Her fingers raced to keep up as the pencil took on a life of its own.

Eric finally noticed her actions. He crouched down beside her. The bedroom had taken on a cozy feel with the two of them working so closely together for the past few hours. He was studying her sketchbook, a frown wrinkling his brow.

He glanced up at her, his frown deepening. "You don't need to look at your creation while you're drawing anymore?"

"What?" Storey glanced down at the page and gasped. "Oh good Lord."

Her hand moved across the page at a mad pace, but she wasn't the one controlling it. At least she didn't think she was drawing right now. Her hand and even her forearm felt separate, unhinged at the elbow from the rest of her. Sketching so fast, she couldn't track the lines as they formed. "Wow," she whispered.

"Double wow." They both stared in awe as the picture became a photographic image of the stylus. "Have you ever done this before?"

"Never."

In silence, they watched and waited for her hand to stop. Her arm dropped to her side and she could now see the whole picture. Her eyes widened. "The stylus has colored ink?"

He snorted. "The stylus doesn't have any ink."

Storey gulped. "Holy crap." She stretched her fingers. They weren't even sore.

"And now what?"

She stared at him and gulped louder. "I'm not sure." Her eyes were drawn back down to the picture. She reached out with her left hand to touch the incredible likeness, only to back off at the last minute, laughing nervously. "I'm scared to try."

Eric stood up and strode over to the window. "We're going to be hunted down and captured, locked away and maybe killed. We should be running to the other side of the planet. Instead, you're drawing pictures that scare you." He shook his head. "I don't understand you."

"But do you get this?" Jubilation rang in her voice.

He spun around to stare at her in complete exasperation. "What? Do I get what?" His gaze landed on the object in her hand. His jaw dropped open. "What the hell?"

Storey stared in shock then gave him a fat grin, almost bouncing on the bed in joy. "You swore. *Finally.* Good for you."

He stared at her uncomprehending. "What are you talking about?"

"You. You swore."

"Swore?" His eyes widened as he shifted his stance and fisted his hands on his hips. "I did not. I couldn't have."

Her grin warped into a smirk as she watched his reaction. "Oh yes, you did. You said, 'What the hell.'"

His face froze. She laughed in delight.

Glaring at her, he said, "That's hardly the issue right now. We have something more important at stake here."

Smirking, she held up the second pencil. "I think this is beyond cool."

"Do you think it works?"

"That it comes off the paper at all is a blooming miracle.

I highly doubt that it's a stylus. I wasn't even thinking of creating a usable one, only a fake one for your people to take off of me, allowing me to keep the real one."

His gaze switched from her left hand to her right hand and back again. "They're identical."

"In appearance," she cautioned, twisting the new pencil around and around. "This isn't even flat like the paper. It's 3D. Unbelievable."

She reached over to hold the new pencil under the light from the lamp at her night table. Sure enough the wording lit up under the warm glow. "Wow. They're perfect copies."

"How did you do that?"

She shrugged. "I'm not sure. I thought about creating a copy of the stylus. The stylus took over and created it for me."

"Can we test it?"

"Why not?" She reached for the sketchbook and tried to draw a line. Nothing. She sat back, disappointed despite her expectations. Pursing her lips, she said, "I didn't really think it would work. The real stylus has a power of some kind. This is a flat carbon copy."

"This just might work...with two styluses you have a chance." He ran his fingers through his hair. Poor Eric. For the first time, real hope glimmered in his eyes. His world had flipped these last few hours. That his father was bent on having her killed was one thing, almost understandable given his people's fears, but to have a kill order on his own head if he didn't comply...now that had to hurt. How would she feel if her father sentenced her to death?

"And you'd care?" She couldn't help asking. What did he really feel? Guilty, because he'd taken her over there in the first place? Or did he feel that same connectedness she felt?

"Huh?" Confused exasperation slid through his voice. "I wouldn't be here otherwise."

She stared at the floor, a giddy ripple snaking through her body. Maybe he did care. Not that she'd let him know it mattered. "So, we're good to go?"

He stared at her. "I still don't like it, but yes, let's get moving. The sooner we get there, the sooner we can find a solution to this mess."

Storey couldn't stop her biggest worry from dominating her thoughts. *What if the solution was one that didn't allow either of them to live?*

STOREY AND ERIC used her drawings to cross the veil to Eric's world. With his guidance, they crossed via Stanshor mine.

"You're sure this is the best entrance?"

"Yes. It used to be a central meeting point for various city members. They'd travel here via codex," he said, holding up his wrist. A long metal band covered his skin from elbow to wrist, "and then come to the hall as a group." He strode into the murky depths of the cavern she'd been happy to forget. He stopped ahead of her and pointed at the ground. "Why did you do this?"

Storey paused to stare at the crosses she'd marked on that fateful day. Had it only been yesterday? Or the day before? She shook her head. Her sense of time had warped. For the first time, she wondered at the long-term side effects and health problems of crossing the veil multiple times. "I was trying to mark out distances, so I'd be able to find my way back again."

"Smart."

There it went again. That little wiggle inside. Damned if she knew why she should care about what he thought of her. She followed him through the darkness to a destination only Eric appeared to know. Storey peered through the blackness, yet saw nothing. He glanced from time to time at his codes. "Is that like a GPS or something?"

"GPS? I don't understand."

"Hmmm." Rather than try to explain something she didn't perfectly understand, she asked, "How does the codex work?"

"It's a digital map, I guess you could say. You can punch in coordinates or places and it can tell you where you are and direct you to a specific place."

"So you just dial up Earth 2.0 and it sends you to a doorway?" She bumped into his back. He held the flashlight in front of him, lighting the immediate space. Everything else appeared to be absolute darkness. "Oomph."

He reached around and grabbed her hand, pulling her up beside him without slowing his pace. Keeping her hand in his, he answered, "Kinda. But a lot more complicated than that. With it I can also create a doorway if I need to in an emergency, and it can send me across my world instantly."

"Perfect way to evade capture."

"Not really. It leaves a signature that is automatically tracked by Paxton's computers. Wherever I go, they'll know."

She frowned. "Okay, not so great."

"We're here." Eric stopped on the spot, showing her the flashing colors on his codex.

She stared at it in disbelief then looked around, "That's it? Just because the colors are different, you're willing to trust that little piece of technology. Look around you. We're nowhere." Her voice rose at the end and it was all she could do to stop herself from yelling. "That's a whole lot of trust in nothing." Her voice echoed on for a long time. She shivered, staring out into black soup that thickened and darkened even as she watched.

"It's all right. Everything's going to be fine." He wrapped one arm around her shoulder and pulled her closer. She didn't protest. In fact, she couldn't resist snuggling up to his comforting warmth. The place gave her the creeps.

"Right," she muttered. "So now what?"

"What do you mean?"

She shuddered again. "Why is it so cold all of a sudden? And what do you mean, what do I mean?" she said in exasperation. "Honestly, sometimes I think you're from another world."

"Well technically…"

With a look of disgust she tried to search her surroundings. The soup had blanketed out everything but Eric, and that's only because she was right beside him.

She shivered. "How do we leave then? I'd like to get out of this."

"That should happen in about five, four, three…"

She reared back. "What the–"

Blue sky beamed down on her.

ERIC REALIZED HE hadn't considered what the transit must have seemed like for her. Everything in her world was so visual. Billboards, television, trains. And everything took so much time. Look at the long hours he'd been forced to attend her school. What a joke. School on his side of the veil was mornings only. And still they finished in half the time that her school system did. Plus, from what he could see, his schooling system taught the youngsters so much more.

That's not to say there weren't some good things over there, he admitted to himself.

"We're here? Just like that?"

"Yes. That's why the darkness thickened and swirled around us. You felt the cold because you haven't had a chance to adapt. I'm used to traveling that way and no longer notice the temperature change."

She sniffed the fresh air while he watched. Did it smell the same to her? Cleaner? Fresher? Foreign? Her features shifted and she seemed to take gulping breaths – almost tasting the air. Curious, he watched the expressions flit across her face. What was she thinking?

"Do you have any pollution here?" She spun around studying the terrain. "Do you have cars? Trains?" She tilted her head back and stared up at the sky. "Airplanes?" With a funny sound that was a cross between a laugh and snort, she added, "Do you even have clouds here? The blue sky looks painted on, it's so perfect."

Spinning around, she tried to take it all in. Her hair flew out in all directions, her t-shirt twisting snugly around her body. Tall compared to the girls he knew, she had an unconscious beauty she made no attempt to capitalize on. Odd, yet endearing. He grinned. Such inquisitiveness. "We don't need those kinds of transportation because everyone has variations of the codex."

"Everything is so different but so much the same."

"Exactly. We as a people developed separately, biologically, environmentally, and socially. Our government structure is completely unique. We don't even have bicycles."

"Don't need them either, do you. Everyone has a codex?"

He watched the unformed queries blaze in her dark chocolate eyes as they darted from one thing to another. "No," he corrected patiently. "They have different units, called taprins, that can take them to any of the many transit points we use. Then everyone walks from there. But those units are only good for local travel."

"Cool. I like the sound of that."

He grinned at her, loving the innocence mingled with eagerness. She had something he hadn't recognized before. What he'd taken as aggressiveness, or maybe *stubbornness* was a better word, was actually spirit. So unlike the girls in his world, who were quiet, graceful, yet contained. They didn't need to be high-spirited. Their lives were easy, peaceful, ordered. But they lacked the spontaneity he'd come to appreciate from Storey.

Another difference between the girls he knew and Storey was her mind. Hers raced and bounced off different things, stopping to question anything of interest before zipping forward. He admired her. He also liked her. That she was seemingly unaware of her physical appeal made her even more unusual. His brief stint at her school showed the females of her age wore tight clothing, bright colored paint on their faces and decorations in their ears, nose, even eyebrows. Storey wore nothing like that. Through confidence or disdain, he didn't know. It set her apart. She made no attempt to attract males. In fact, she ignored them all equally.

Except maybe…him. That he enjoyed her, respected her…and dare he say…cared for her, was a big surprise he hadn't considered prior to taking this job. He didn't see how she could be part of his future, yet he already knew there'd be a gaping hole in his life if she wasn't.

"Which way?" Storey waved her arms at the multiple paths stretching out before them.

Eric studied the bright green and yellow bushes adding a cheerful look to the early morning. Given the number of choices, he quickly picked one of the least traveled paths. They needed to stay under cover as long as they could.

He glanced around, realizing they could be pounced on by guards at any time. "This way."

CHAPTER 11

STOREY FOLLOWED AS Eric hurried toward the trees ahead. He'd gone from standing around to full speed. Weird.

She made it seconds after him. Still gasping at the unexpected pace, she grabbed his arm, barely slowing him down. "What's the panic?"

He twisted to look down at her, that sideways grin sliding her way. "I just remembered that people could be looking for us. Here we are, standing around like ducks in hunting season."

A horrible comparison. She shuddered. At least she now knew they had ducks and a hunting season.

Brushing back the green overgrowth, Eric trotted ahead. "We'll enter the city by the back gates."

"Aren't they guarded?" She hurried to catch him. His long legs ate up the miles, leaving her sputtering in shock. Normally, she let other people eat *her* dirt.

"Not by people," he said.

Wincing, she decided not to ask. She'd find out soon enough. "How much further?"

"Half an hour, give or take." He headed off again at a quick clip. "Or less, if you'd move a little faster."

After that comment, she jogged to keep up. Focused on trying to maintain his grueling pace, she slammed into him when he came to a sudden stop.

"What's wrong," she gasped, staggering back several steps to bend over and catch her breath. She closed her eyes briefly. Damn, she'd developed a stitch in her side. Eric wasn't even out of breath.

"We're here."

Thank heavens for that. Straightening, she surveyed the immediate area. Where was here? What could he see that she didn't? Thick evergreens clogged her view on one side. Not big fat trunks of an old growth forest, but thousands of skinny trees so crowded together she could barely see through them. Everywhere else appeared to be open field. No building. No fence. And certainly no gate. "What am I looking at?"

"A forest?" Again that superior amusement. It was really starting to piss her off. Glad he thought her ignorance was so funny. Not.

She shot him a disgusted look. "Yeah. I can see that. What about your gate?"

"It's on the other side of this group over there." He pointed out the trees in question.

"Is your codex telling you that again?" She shielded her eyes from the bright light to stare where he pointed. It didn't help.

"And the fact that I've been here before." He walked toward the invisible gate, a happy bounce to his step.

She wished she had the same endurance. This last leg of the trip had tired her. The stitch in her side still irritated. Several steps later, she slowed as the blinding sun darkened. The air had taken on a static emptiness, a weird sense of something missing. Shivers slid down her back. "Hey, Eric. What's with the change in light?"

"It's a standard gate warning for anyone approaching. It means we're here."

"Warning? I don't like the sound of that."

"Normal for here and not a big deal if you follow the safeguards."

"Whoa. What safeguards? What are you talking about?" She cast a quick look behind her. She couldn't shake the feeling of being watched. "Hey, wait up."

"I'm here."

"Not here enough." The blackness swirled around her, making her choke with the thickness of it. She reached out for Eric. He pulled her closer. She gasped and pressed tight against his side. "Don't you dare let go. I hate this."

He chuckled, his warmth breath tickling her cheek. She had to smile. "No worries. Stay close."

She snorted. "You think?" She twisted around, that eerie sensation crawling up her back again. Tugging, she tried to get him to move. He planted his feet and resisted.

"What is your problem?" he burst out in exasperation.

"Something is watching us."

He stilled. "What are you talking about?"

Peering up at him through the deepening mist, she tried to understand the odd flatness in his voice. "Don't you feel it?"

"What? Feel eyes on us?"

"Yes." She searched the suffocating blackness. "As long as I can't see them, they can't see me. Right?" she joked.

"In theory. Besides we're in the gate. Nothing can get us in here." He wrapped his arms around her to pull her close. She huddled in his arms, her eyes darting in all directions.

Her stomach was in knots. So were her nerves. "What kind of animals do you have over here?"

"All kinds of them." His grin flashed in the dark.

"That's not helping. Animal predators?"

His warm chuckle lifted the hair at her temple, sending a different sensation down her spine. "Of course. You're really spooked, aren't you?"

Lifting her head, she stared up at his laughing blue eyes. Here heart tumbled. She sighed. "Am I overreacting?"

His chest rumbled against her. "No, not when it's all new to you."

She dropped her forehead against him for a moment, then she asked, "Is the gate like the one in the mine?"

"Sort of."

"Why can't you give me something other than half an answer?" She'd barely finished when a scream sounded next to her. She half climbed Eric's tall frame. "What the hell was that?"

Clasping her tightly to his chest, he whispered into her ear, "Shhhh. An animal hunting. That's all. Quiet."

She stilled. Her heart in her throat, her nerves quietly shattered while her eyes stared into the damn soup. Her nose quivered.

"Just another minute more." This time the warmth of his voice wafted against her neck. She shuddered. Eric almost made her forget her surroundings. He squeezed her tighter. Going on instinct, she snuggled closer.

This was his world. She had no way of defending herself. She didn't even know what dangers existed. She'd never felt so helpless in her life.

"Hmmm."

Regret nudged her when she realized Eric's arms were loosening. She lifted her head and looked around, hoping for the blue sky again. Not happening. Black, cloying night surrounded them. She swallowed loudly. "Didn't it work? Is this where we're supposed to be?"

Eric stared down at his codex. "I'm not sure. The codex is flashing that we've arrived."

"Arrived where? It doesn't look any different from before." She waited for the dense fog to clear. It didn't. "Is your codex broken?"

"Not likely. It worked fine up until now."

She didn't like the confusion on his face. The silence around them had a muffled sensation to it. Not a clear air type of silence, more of a padded chamber type of thing. "Did it though? You said you'd been here before. Have you physically been at this gate before?"

He didn't answer.

"You haven't, have you?" She couldn't believe it. He'd duped her. "So how do you know if any of this is right?" she exclaimed, frustration stiffening her backbone. She pulled back slightly to stare up at him.

"I've seen pictures of this place. I've studied the area and the gate itself." He tried to pull her closer. She resisted, wanting to read the truth in his eyes. "This should have passed by now. But then, all gates take a different amount of time. This one could be slower."

"It's not slower." She knew it, and again had no idea how or why. "Something is wrong."

"Not yet it isn't."

"If… something has gone wrong, where would this wrong be?"

"Huh?"

"Where would we be if the gate didn't work?"

He frowned. "I don't know. It's never happened before."

She disengaged from his grasp, turning to look around at

the heavy charcoal colored mist. Better than cloying blackness, but not by much. She wafted the mist around, hoping to clear some of it. "Never? Or never to you?"

"Never that I know of."

"What are the probable things that could go wrong with your codex?"

"Like dialing the wrong number you mean? Nothing like that. Each is a preset code." His eyes widened. Reaching out, he grabbed her hand. "Stay close."

"Could the numbers have been changed? Like by Paxton?"

He frowned. "I don't know. The codes are old. Well before his time."

"But it's possible. And, I'm just thinking aloud here, is it possible that we're in some kind of middle zone? No man's land? A different dimension again?"

"I really don't know." He spun around to look behind him, then turned back to face her. "We could be at a different gate. Lost between gates even. Like I said, it's never happened before."

"Well," she suggested, "why don't you dial your codex and take us back to Stanshor Mine and we'll try a different, more traveled route."

Understanding brightened his eyes. He lifted his wrist. No lights flashed. Nothing glowed. Grim-faced, he tapped several buttons. "Now it's not working at all, apparently."

Her stomach sank. Of course it wasn't. They weren't meant to go back. "Could Paxton have done this on purpose or could something else have gone wrong that would change the codes?"

"What could go wrong? Nothing goes wrong in my home." He winced. "Although my people might say losing the stylus was wrong. But only that." He rushed to say.

They stared at each other, puzzled. Then it hit them.

"The Louers!" they cried.

Storey's mind went blank, just for a moment, then raced ahead. The possibility that they'd arrived in the middle of a war was too much to contemplate.

Cautiously, Eric spoke as the voice of reason. "Let's not jump to conclusions. That's only one possibility."

"True." She nodded at his codex. "First things first. Do you have a way to get us out of here?"

Glaring down at the codex, Eric's frown deepened. "I don't know. Outside of trying to walk out of this."

"Which may or may not work. So…" She pulled out her sketchbook and stylus. "Where should we go? To my world or deeper into yours? Are we thinking Louers have invaded? Or are we thinking Paxton did this to stop you from going home?" She stared up at him. He stared back, an odd look on his face. "Hey, are you in there?" she snapped her fingers in front of his face. "Pull it together. We're in trouble here, in case you didn't notice."

"Let me reset my codex. Could be just a glitch?" He tapped a series of buttons again while Storey watched. Frowning, he studied his codex and the unchanging mist around them. "What's the chance it needs another minute? A reboot so to speak."

She snorted. "Get a grip. The gate is either not functioning or this *is* the destination. Either way, I'm not impressed." She plopped cross-legged on the ground. It didn't look like dirt or tile, more like black compressed nothing. Refusing to dwell on it, she opened her sketchbook and flipped to a new page. Her mind raced, searching for possibilities. After her one horrible encounter with the Louers, she'd hate for the same nightmare to take over Eric's world. Just because his father was an asshole, that didn't mean everyone else was.

"What are you doing?" He squatted down beside her.

"I'm trying to figure out where we should go. What if the Louers have entered your world? Do you want to help your people? Haven't you imagined them tearing into your friends' homes and attacking your family?" She stared down at the sketch forming under her fingers. The stylus had warmed, heating with an urgency all its own.

"I don't have any friends." His voice held a cool indifference.

She looked up, startled. "What?"

"I said I don't have any friends. I have teammates, coworkers, associates. No friends. Everyone in my world is part of my work."

"Girlfriends?"

"Not really." Short and curt. Hmmm. Some history there, but not her place to ask. And she didn't think she wanted to know. "Didn't you make any friends through work?" Most people made friends with their coworkers. After all, that's where most people spent the bulk of their waking hours. It only made sense that strong friendships would form during this time.

He shrugged. "My father."

"Yeah, I can see how he'd put a damper on things. I have to admit my mother and her little candle shop have certainly brought me grief." She returned to her drawing, her mind a muddle of remembered grievances with the townsfolk. Her poor mom was harmless. So what if her store was new-agey and her religion was different. *He* had no friends? Yeah, well, she could relate.

"He's not all bad."

"No one is." She could feel his stare and ignored it as the picture emerged from the sketchpad. Paxton's lab. She sighed. Talk about walking back into a lion's den.

Eric studied the picture taking shape. "Paxton is a good man. He's a government man who cares about my people. About me. He's trained me for the last decade, longer even."

"Decade?" She shot him a questioning glance before returning to her picture. "Sounds like he's been more of a father to you than your own father."

"That's true." He reached across and tapped the paper. "You're thinking to go back to Paxton's lab? Did you forget there's a death sentence on your head?"

She sighed. "No, I haven't forgotten that. I hate to say it, but I'm thinking they may have more important things to worry about now."

"If they do, they might consider you responsible."

She stared at him in dismay. "See, that's the problem with you guys. You just don't want to accept responsibility for your own actions. This isn't all about me. This is about you and your people. Remember, I didn't sneak into your world and leave you an innocent-looking bomb to play with."

He grinned and shook his head. "I can see your point. However, just because *I* might understand, doesn't mean the others are going to be so open."

She snorted. "Well, they damn well better be. This is a result of their actions. The buck stops with them." Her hand stopped. She studied the finished picture with a critical eye. "I suppose that's close enough. I suggest we do a second picture. I don't know. Possibly of the same mine again, so that we can step into Paxton's lab and check out the climate, then if the Louers are trying to take the place over, we can use the second picture as an escape route. This way we'll have enough for both of us to carry – in case we get separated."

He nodded, apparently content to just watch. "That was the original plan anyway, right?"

"Kinda." She sketched quickly, her hand a blur, until she was satisfied with the second drawing. She had to admit that the stylus had improved her artistic ability tenfold. "That should do it. Now let's go."

He stood up and held out a hand for her. "You first."

"No, I think we'd better go together."

"We won't fit. You made complete doors, not partial ones that suggest bigger ones."

"True, but, as I'm learning I'm finding it's more about what you're thinking than the actual size of the drawing.

He stared at her, dumfounded. "Huh?"

"Don't worry about it. Come on."

She ripped off the first page. "How can I go through and take the paper with me?"

"Like I did in the lab. Just grab it on the way through."

She placed the sketch on the ground and motioned for him to step onto it. Casually, like it was every day event, Eric stepped through and disappeared from sight. She shook her head. There's no way she was *ever* going to get used to that.

Taking a deep breath, she knelt on the paper keeping a firm grip on the corner with her hand. She fell through.

Tumbling into Paxton's lab, she groaned as she smacked into the hard white tile. Kneeling wasn't a good idea. Then again, as she surveyed the paper in her hand with satisfaction, it allowed her to bring the gate with her.

"That wasn't very graceful." Eric's voice was a little fuzzy.

Struggling to her feet, Storey turned to face him. "It also gave me a hell of a headache."

Eric stood, legs straddled, hands on his hips, staring at her. "You've crossed through a lot of doors recently, some damage is possible."

She shot him a worried look. "What kind of damage?" Shaking her head, she added, "Never mind. Don't tell me. I can't do anything about it now." She spun around, realizing that the room was empty. "Is this Paxton's lab? If so, then where is he?"

Eric walked around, opening doors then closing them after checking the rooms on the other side. "He's always here. We'll have to go looking for him."

"Where does he live? He must eat and sleep somewhere else?"

"Yes, but he lives here most of the time." Eric fisted his hands on his hips. "He should be here."

Storey understood. War, and all that it entailed, wasn't part of Eric's thought process. He'd never encountered it. Didn't live with the possibility every day, like her people did. He had no idea of what was going on here.

There was no point explaining things to him. He'd have to sort through this on his own, eventually.

It wasn't for her to tell him that his peaceful world was under attack.

CHAPTER 12

S TOREY HEADED FOR the last door.

Eric reached it ahead of her and opened it. "There should be lights on." He scanned the room before crossing past the big oval table and to the door on the far end. Storey followed.

The meeting chamber didn't appear to have been used since she'd been here last. Cups and bottles littered the table and the chairs sat everywhere, as if pushed back in a hurry. It was consistent with an emergency meeting having been called or everyone having left at a run.

Eric disappeared into the next room. Only it wasn't a room at all, but a long hallway with doors set off each other in military precision for as far as Storey could see. The floor gleamed in white tile. The walls and ceiling sparkled in winter white, almost blinding her. Nothing but black hardware marred the pristine color.

"What's with all the white?"

"White is a power color here." He came to a stop at the third door on the left. He knocked.

The doors reached from floor to ceiling. Storey couldn't help comparing the building to an institution of locked cells. There was a real creepiness to the emptiness. "If there were people walking around, the place wouldn't be quite so off-putting."

He turned to give her a curious glance, then pushed open the door, calling out, "Paxton, are you in here?"

No answer. He poked his head around the corner of the door and called out louder, "Paxton?"

The stillness of a place that should have been teeming with activity gave her the willies. "It's not Sunday, is it?"

Eric pushed the door fully open, then paused to look back at her. "You ask the darnedest questions. What does Sunday have to do with it?"

"I don't know. I just thought that if it were Sunday, then it would make sense that no one was here. If you have church, that is? Or if it were night time? Could everyone be asleep? Are we even on the same clock?" She couldn't stop asking questions. Besides it would help take his mind off things.

His lips quirked. "Remember, we're still on the same planet. Same solar system. If it's daytime on one side of the veil, it's daytime on the other. It is Sunday, although we call it something slightly different here." His face became serious again. "But even on Council days, this building is always manned."

He walked through what appeared to be a small apartment, heading for the far side of the room. There was a weird set of cushions on the floor. Furniture of some kind. As she passed it, her leg accidentally brushed the edge and it moved. She jumped back, shrieking, her hand slamming against her chest. The pillows rose and adjusted, almost as if it were fitting to her size.

Eric snickered. "No church. No religion as you know it. The Council sets the rules for everything." His grin widened. "And we don't have time to play with the chairs."

Giving the piece a wide berth, she glared at him. "I don't

consider a cushion that looks like it's going to eat me as funny, thank you."

"That's a polo chair." At her blank look, he added, "One size fits all."

She gave the cushion one last assessing look, realizing it had shrunk back down to its original size. Handy. The next room appeared to be a bedroom. She wandered around. What else was different over here? The bed looked normal, although higher than she was used to, with a small set of stairs on the side. No headboard, but a control panel of some kind had been mounted on the wall above some more weird looking pillows. She stayed well away from it, just in case it moved, too.

Everything was white.

Glancing down at her black jeans, black boots and her charcoal t-shirt, she realized she looked and felt like a dandelion among the roses.

Eric checked out the room and stood in the doorway of another room. She could only surmise that it was a bathroom of some kind. Not that she'd seen anything along those lines since she'd been here. As soon as the thought crossed her mind, she realized she needed to pee. *Damn.*

She headed in the same direction Eric had disappeared. It wasn't a bathroom. It appeared to be another workroom. "What on earth? Why would he have another lab here?"

"This is his private space. And the one other place I expected to find him." He ran his fingers through his hair in frustration. "Paxton doesn't *go* anywhere else. He can't. Where the hell can he be?"

"He *can't* go anywhere? Ever?" She studied the all white and silver room, so painfully clean she had to resist the urge to toss a cabinet to make it look normal.

"No. You don't understand. He doesn't do well in the outside – something to do with his extreme age."

"How old is he?"

"No one really knows. He won't talk about it. Somewhere between one-fifty and two hundred."

Storey choked. "Two hundred. What is the life expectancy of your people?"

He frowned. "Same as your people, I imagine. Although, we've stopped disease and slowed aging, so maybe not."

She blinked. "Did you say stopped? You mean you wiped those two things out? We could sure use that technology. We live to seventy or eighty and anyone who makes it over one hundred is considered ancient."

A weird crack sounded in the other room.

Pushing her behind him, Eric held his finger to his lips and motioned her back to the main living room. He snuck up to the doorway and peered inside. Something crashed to the floor in the other room.

"Crap. What was that?" she whispered, racing to his side.

"Get down." He yanked her behind the wall. "Are you nuts?" He stood up and peered around the corner. "Whoever it was is gone." Racing to the window on the far wall, he searched the outside grounds.

"A window?" She laughed and ran to his side. "That's the first one I've seen here. I wondered if you had them."

He shot another strange look in her direction. "You're really odd, you know. Come on. We have to continue searching." His voice had chilled. "Someone has to be left around here."

Storey followed in silence as Eric strode from door to door, opening each and every one, calling out constantly. No one answered. The place, the whole huge mausoleum, was empty.

"Do you guys have an underground bunker, a safe room, or something?"

"Not if you mean like a place to hide when under attack. Remember, we don't have wars. This is extremely unusual."

That's not the word she'd have used. But if this problem sidelined the death sentence on her head, she was all for it. She stood in the hallway and waited as he finished checking each door. Nothing. "Now what?"

"We're going to my place."

She perked up. "How far away?"

"Only a couple of minutes."

"Oh good. Do you have bathrooms here?"

He winced. "Of course. You are so weird."

"I'm weird. Look at the way you're acting. I'd have contacted the people I care about to make sure they were safe then I would check the media for updates. The Internet would be teeming with news. Look at you. You don't even know where to look. Do you have media here? Computers? Internet? Phones? How much research did you have to do to blend into my world?"

She was almost shouting by the time she finished, struggling to keep up with him as he followed a series of twists and turns. He came to standstill in front of yet another white door. It opened on its own.

"How'd you do that?"

"It's my apartment." He shot her a puzzled look. "Why wouldn't it open for me?"

"Gee, I don't know, maybe because you didn't open it with your hand."

"I don't need to, it's tuned to my vibration."

She nodded. "Yup. I can see how that might work. Not."

She walked into another sparse, almost utilitarian type of apartment. Eric's had even less furniture than Paxton's rooms, and it was equally as nondescript. There was no personality here. Nothing on the walls to liven things up. If she lived here, the first thing she'd do is get out her paint brush and color the world.

"How long have you lived here?"

"Again with the questions. Since I was old enough to live on my own."

Sensing this might answer a lot of questions, she asked, "How long ago was that and how old were you?"

"The same age as everyone else. Fourteen."

She sucked in her cheeks. The same as everyone else. So at fourteen, everyone in his world was independent. She kind of liked that. "How old are you?"

"A couple of years older than you. I think Paxton said you were what, sixteen, seventeen?"

"Yes, just turning seventeen." A loud buzzer sounded. Relief washed over his face. He raced to the far wall and placed his hand on a circle looking thing. A large screen materialized, taking up most of the wall at his head height.

"Greetings, Eric."

"What's going on? Where is everyone?" Eric stared into the blue screen. Standing beside him, Storey couldn't see anything but a blue snow. She had no idea who he was speaking with.

"We're under attack. Central is on lockdown." A computerized voice gave a general status report. Understanding filled Eric's face. "Who's attacking? We've never even had enemies before."

Storey winced at the shock in his voice. She already knew the answer.

"The Louers are attacking."

THE BLUE SCREEN died. Eric yelled, shoving his face right up to the monitor. "No, wait! I need more information. Where are you?"

The reception blinked off and on, then a cracked voice said, "Mansfield gate has been reopened."

Eric blinked. "Mansfield?" he whispered. Fear settled at his feet. It couldn't be. He raised his voice. "That's not a real place – is it?"

The static on the screen increased, drowning out the computerized transmission.

"Now that's a weird phone."

He spun, having forgotten she was standing beside him. "It's not a telephone. The visual is broken, that's all."

"So how do we get to Mansfield?"

No way. She couldn't go with him. She shouldn't be here now. The whole game had changed. This was no longer about saving the two of them; it was about saving his people and their way of life. "Not we, me. My country is at war. You shouldn't be here. Go home and stay there. Look for a place to hide over there, just in case. You might be lucky and the Louers will be too busy here to worry about attacking your world."

She made that cute little sound again. The one that was a cross between disbelief and thinking he was an ass. It had grown on him. Like she had. And that was dangerous. He had to help his people. He couldn't afford to be distracted.

"They already have, remember?"

"Not like this." He spun around, wondering if he needed anything before he left to find the rest of his countrymen.

Distracted, he said, "Look I can't worry about that right now. I have to find the others. I wish Paxton was here. He'd know what to do."

"You need to go wherever you're supposed to go during lockdown."

He stared at her in confusion.

"He said Central was under lockdown," she said.

His confusion cleared. Right. Lockdown procedures. He'd been so caught up with the Mansfield gate news. "There's a second base in the basement. It's just never been used."

"Let's go."

"No, you should go home." He hesitated. It wasn't fair, but now that the worst had come to pass she needed to know. "They're going to blame you for this. There's no way they aren't."

"I'm not going there again. I'm not to blame. I contributed, yes. Because I didn't know what I was doing, but now that I do, I might be able to help."

He shook his head vigorously. "They are going to shoot you on sight. You won't get a chance to explain or help. They're going to look for someone to blame. You."

"All right already. Go." She pushed him out the door. "I can get home myself."

"I'll wait until you cross." There's no way he would leave her here alone. Not now. Anything could happen to her. He narrowed his gaze. He couldn't afford to back down on this one.

Storey stood eye-to-eye with him, then weary, she ran a hand through her black hair and eased back. He really wanted to snatch her up into a tight hug at that moment. He didn't dare.

Dropping her backpack to the floor, she pulled out the one sketch from Paxton's lab. "The same architecture has been used on the hallway. I should be able to get home from here."

She placed the picture on the floor and hesitated. Taking a deep breath, she looked at him one last time. "Take care of yourself."

He swallowed hard. The reality that this could be their last meeting settled into his gut. "Wait." He snatched her into his arms and kissed her. Hard. Just like last time, fire licked at his hardening muscles. Lust filled his groin, and the pain of parting filled his heart. He might never see her again.

He tore his lips away before he devoured her on the spot. "Please go home." He stepped back, afraid his legs wouldn't hold him. "I need to know you'll be safe," he said hoarsely.

With a crooked smile and without a sound, she jumped on the picture and through the floor.

She was gone. Just like that.

Bewildered, Eric realized she'd managed to take the picture portal with her again. Unbelievable. How she'd managed to learn so much without training amazed him. Time for her later, at least he hoped so. But not now. He couldn't afford the distraction. Not when his whole world was under attack. He had to find the basement, a place he'd never been.

IT WAS A relief to step into her own bedroom once again. To know that she could get back. Having the portal in here was downright convenient, just not conducive to getting a good night's sleep. Who knew what or who else might crawl through? If only she'd known then what she knew now, she'd have created the portal somewhere else but still close by. Who knew that once opened, the portal was available to anyone from the other side. She needed her picture, but they had codexes and who knew what all else. It would be all too easy to end up trapped in her room. Or worse – wake up with a stranger coming through in the dead of night.

Her fingers stroked her swollen lips. Eric. She hadn't wanted to leave, to leave him. For all the comfort of being home and seeing the same old furniture and purple walls she'd lived with for years, there was no satisfaction to being here.

Dumping her backpack on her bed, she headed for the washroom. At the doorway she stopped, a niggling sensation reminding her she'd yet to be separated from the stylus since this mess had begun. Being apart didn't feel right even now. She ran back, did a quick change of clothes, snagged up her bag, and then headed to the washroom. Downstairs, the evening air had cooled the house. Darkness added to the clamminess, the empty feeling chilling her further. She'd thought her mom would be home by now, but apparently not. She'd traveled to another dimension and back and her mom was still out with her friends. Weird.

Heading to the den, she checked on the wall. And couldn't stifle the sigh of relief that there was no evidence the Louers had tried to break through again. There had to be a way to stop them from coming here permanently. The last thing she wanted was to have to keep an eye on the wall every time she came home.

She only had Eric's word that the Louers were horrible. She needed to stop them from coming into her home, but she didn't want to kill them all off. She didn't even kill spiders. But there had to be a happy solution for everyone here. If only she could find it.

Could she draw a lock on the original door? Or draw another dimension between her world and theirs? Then if they did cross they'd end up in the new place and not know there were more dimensions. Did just drawing something like that make it so? That brought her back full circle; just what capabilities did the stylus have?

Retrieving her sketchbook from her room, she decided to find out.

She pulled up the old rocker, turned on the pole lamp and sat facing the repaired wall. Figuring out a solution could take some time. Would the stylus figure it out for her? She held the thought of a permanent solution, of a locking system and a dimension between her world and theirs, then let the stylus work.

If the Louers found a better world than hers, they might be happy there and look no further. Her world *was* lovely. So, theoretically theirs would be too. They might find it like a holiday resort, compared to their current living standard. Something she knew nothing about. Again, she had only Eric's word that the Louers were the bad guys – but if they *were* like locusts, destroying everything in their path, then she wanted to make sure they stayed a long ways away from her world.

Not realizing what she was doing on a conscious level, she rocked gently in the chair as her hand flashed and dipped, crossed and slashed through its creation process.

She closed her eyes and leaned her head back. How she could do this without looking she didn't know. Still, she was so tired…and she let the room slip away.

The front door opened a little later. Storey recognized the familiar sound of her mom's return. Damn. She rubbed her eyes with her left hand. Moonlight poured into the dark room, lighting her sketchbook. The stylus was still busy creating. She didn't want to stop. This was too important.

Her mom walked through to the kitchen. "The power is out, Anton."

It was? The power had gone out and she hadn't noticed? Had she actually slept? Then the rest of her mother's words registered. Storey stiffened, her eyes widened even as bile rose up the back of her throat. *Anton?* Her father? No way.

The deep male voice made her heart beat a jungle roll in her chest.

"Probably just a breaker. There could have been a power outage, I suppose. I'll go check."

Jesus, it almost sounded like him. At least, as her imagination remembered him. Her dad had left ten years ago. What was he doing here and why would her mother act so…so normal about it all? And how the hell would he know where the breakers were located?

Swallowing heavily, Storey glanced at the clock. She'd been in here for an hour plus. In the dark. "Hi. I'm in the den," she called out.

"What are you doing sitting here all alone with just that little bit of light? Are you okay? And why aren't you in bed asleep?" Her mother entered the room, worry evident in her voice. Storey was sorry for that. She hadn't meant to be such a constant concern.

And there was more to come. She needed a cover story for the cracks in the wall, too. "I'm just sitting here. I couldn't sleep, so I came down to draw, but it's too dark without lights. Weird. Then there was that even weirder tremor, earlier."

"What? An earthquake? We didn't feel a thing." Storey's

mom hurried to her side, placing a hand on her shoulder. "Are you okay? You weren't hurt by it, were you?"

An odd rose perfume wafted over Storey. Strange, she didn't recognize it. "No. Just restless afterwards."

"Oh, dear. You should have called. We'd have come home." Her mother looked around the small room. "I hope there's no damage."

"I couldn't see much with the power outage. Maybe a little cracked paint." Storey grinned in the dark. What a great cover story. And dreamt up in mere seconds.

"As long as you weren't hurt, the rest is nothing. It's probably time to throw up another coat of paint anyway."

Storey smiled.

"What's with your bag?"

That worried note had entered her mother's voice again. Storey glanced down at her backpack, thinking quickly. "It has my art stuff in it."

"Oh." And there, that predictable relief again. Storey didn't think she wanted children if it meant a roller coaster ride of emotions like that. A man walked into the room. Storey stiffened, searching the gloom to see his features.

Her father.

Her heart and mind took an immediate hit. No contact in ten years and now he just walked in like he owned the place. Her eyes locked on him and wouldn't let go. How many times in the last ten years had she wanted, needed to see him again? She gulped softly. Not trusting herself to either slug him or hug him, she chose to stay where she was.

"The tremors must have knocked the power out. There's no phone either. I can go to a neighbor's house to check and see if they have at least a cell phone working or wait until morning. They might have it fixed by then anyway," he said.

Storey's gaze widened. He was acting as if he lived here – the nerve. And how did he know about the neighbors?

"Considering the time, we might as well go to bed. The power will be back on in the morning, I'm sure."

Storey wasn't. Her world had been rocked several times tonight. Her hand still sketched at a mad pace under the cover of darkness. She needed to finish. Soon. At some point, exhaustion would take over. Mental chaos had begun to move in. At least there was no room for the nagging doubt about leaving Eric and his people alone to fight this war.

"Storey, are you going to bed now? You have school to-morrow."

"It's a school day tomorrow?" It felt like Saturday. But then Eric had said it was Sunday. Crap. She was twisted up time-wise, as well. *Damn.*

"No, Sarah. Remember, she has the day off."

Storey stared at him in the dark. She did? She didn't remember that. Good thing the lighting hid her expression. Besides, how would he know?

"Oh that's right," Her mother turned back to face Sto-rey. "She was supposed to go on that religion field trip. Like we would want you learning about other religions. We're Roman Catholics all the way."

Religion field trip? Roman Catholic? Uh oh! Who'd sto-len her mom and put these fakes in her place? Storey didn't know what to say. Something major had happened. Not to her, but to her family.

"Are you two feeling all right?"

"I'm not too sure." Her mother rubbed her forehead. "In fact, I'm starting to feel slightly woozy. I think I'd better go to bed." She traipsed out of the room. Storey couldn't believe what she saw briefly in the ray of moonlight. Her mother wore a dress, like a regular dress and high heels. That so didn't happen. Where were the floor length hippy dresses and bangles that jangled with her movements?

"Where were you guys? You mentioned it earlier, but I forgot."

Her father spoke from the doorway. "At church, of course. We understood you needed to stay home and do your homework. That's always been your priority and we're so proud of you for it. Now don't stay up too late." He walked out, leaving her stunned and gasping for air.

What had just happened? If these were her parents, then they weren't in her normal world. Had she returned to her world or had she gone to a different one?

She glanced down at her drawing. Could she have done this? Could she possibly have created another dimension? Another reality? A parallel reality? She got up, still holding the stylus and sketchbook, to check the wall where the Louer had tried to come through earlier. Relief washed through her. The cracked paint was still there. Evidence she was in the right dimension.

Unless that had copied over too…

Oh God.

Please not. And if she had copied an entire world, which one was she in now?

<h1 style="text-align:center">Chapter 13</h1>

ERIC TRIED TO remember the emergency instructions drilled into him during his first years of training. Like so much of his early learning, his training had been mindless rote instructions, ignored the minute the tests were over. There'd never been a conflict or a war in their immediate history and no one had considered the possibility of a fight in their future.

They'd been so wrong.

He had yet to see any Louers, and his images of war, gleaned from the archives, had all focused on screaming crowds and bloodshed everywhere, fighting and chaos erupting on every corner. This deathly silence didn't fit the image.

Making it to the ground floor, he wasted more precious minutes looking for the entrance to the basement. The steel door stood implacable in front of him. It wouldn't be automatically keyed for him and he couldn't remember the codes to get in.

Damn it.

Shocked at the swearing, even silent curses, he stepped back. Storey's bad habit was rubbing off on him. Not good.

He massaged his temples and tried several combinations in his head. As soon as the right one showed up the door should click open. Numbers flitted in and out in a steady stream as he reviewed the various codes he'd been forced to memorize throughout his life.

The massive door made a series of clicking noises and unlocked itself. Relief washed over him. He pulled the door open. With a final glance around at the deserted hallway, he entered the darkness.

STOREY SAT FROZEN, ever nastier possibilities filling her mind. All thoughts about returning to Eric's world fled as she realized she had to put her own reality back to rights. How? She had no frickin' idea.

Lost in thought, she didn't recognize for a long moment that her hand had stopped moving. The stylus was done. She gathered up her bag and slipped up the stairs to her room. Not wanting to attract her parent's attention she quietly shut the door and slipped into her bed. Under the covers she used her flashlight to study her drawing. She didn't quite understand what she was looking at. The picture appeared to be earth displayed as an onion with multiple layers wrapped on top of each other. Were the layers dimensions? Had she created a layer here? She'd wondered about it but...

She grabbed her school eraser and scrubbed at the center layer. It wouldn't erase. Changing tactics, she worked on a smaller mark on one of the outer layers. Again, she couldn't. Were these creations permanent?

Sick awareness settled into her gut. What had she been thinking about while drawing? So many things. Most recently her parents. Before that, wishing her mom would conform a little more and Eric, well all she'd had on her mind was how she'd hated to leave Eric's arms. After that, her thoughts were consumed with trying to find another dimension for the Louers.

She gulped. Could the power of thought, when paired with a stylus, change a person's belief system? Change their history, too? And those around them? Dear God.

It didn't make sense that she could, without training, change something so drastic, so major in life so easily. And if the changes had happened to her parents, had they also happened to other people? Did her mom still have the candle shop? Did the townsfolk still look down on them? And what about Jeff? Was he or had he ever been her boyfriend? Or had they never met?

Storey gulped. Was she still Storey? She didn't feel any different. But apparently she acted differently in this place. Homework? Caring about her schooling? Nuts. Did she even live in Bankhead anymore?

She ran to the window. The same overgrown oak tree scraped along the sill. Her familiar backyard shimmered in the moonlight. Relief washed over her. So that much was still good. More had to have changed though to have her father in her life, not to mention a change in her mother's religious beliefs. And if her mom's clothing tastes had changed, that meant the alterations were old and very deep.

The power of what she'd done scared the crap out of her. For the first time she understood Paxton's fear. And what was the chance he knew the stylus could change reality like this?

Laying the stylus down on the bed, she sat a little away from it. It had taken a long-held wish and brought her Dad home. It was her fault, she fully accepted that. Now she needed to understand how she'd done this, so she could fix it. Then she'd be more than happy to stop playing God with laws and tools she didn't understand.

Studying the stylus, she had to consider giving it back. "If you're so dangerous, you shouldn't be running around my planet loose like this."

So how did she become one of those in the know?

Then it hit her. If the pencil could change her parents' belief system, then surely it could give her more information – like an instruction manual on using the stylus and information on Eric's world. For that matter, it might be able to tell her how to defeat the Louers.

How could she get the stylus to release the information? Through a drawing? Storey grabbed a granola bar from her bag and munched. She was hesitant to draw herself; who knew if her poor rendition would create that face on her bone and tissue. She could put her name down.

Wincing, she realized that knowing more of the potential disasters she could create made her hesitant to do *anything*. A little information went a long way, and she was terrified of making things worse.

But she had to fix this.

"Stylus, how do I make this all better?" She picked up her pencil and grabbed her sketchbook.

ERIC WALKED THROUGH the darkness, waiting for his eyes to adjust – except they weren't adjusting. Of course, he hadn't thought to bring a light with him. Who'd have thought the basement wouldn't have the same control system as the rest of the building where the lights came on automatically? "Hello? Anyone here?"

Silence.

What if no one had come here? This area appeared to have been closed for decades. Centuries. He stopped, recognizing a wall in the gloom in front of him. He placed a hand on the wall. Relief overwhelmed him when he realized he'd reached another doorway. He searched for the number sequence and managed to retrieve it in half the time. The door opened, light spilling his way.

Thank heavens for that. He stepped around and into the glow.

And stopped in shock.

AS A TEST, she sat crossed-legged on the bed and asked the stylus to give her information on Eric's people in a safe manner. A curious lightness washed over her as her hand moved across the paper. She gave it a moment to do what needed to be done without her mind filling in the pieces, which might or might not affect the picture, she then opened her eyes and looked. The picture appeared to be a large filing cabinet. One drawer was open. The label on the slightly raised file said Eric Stodd's Memories.

Way cool.

She blinked several times and looked around her room. Everything else appeared the same. Placing the tip of the stylus on Eric's file, she closed her eyes and thought about him. Instantly, she could see him running as a child, then scenes started flashing of him in a uniform, first at school then through training. She gasped at the sight of Eric in a clinch with a young woman. Her hand jerked back and the flood of sensual memories stopped. The sense of having invaded Eric's life didn't. She winced. She really hadn't planned for that to happen.

"Oh boy."

So, there *was* more to his girlfriend issue. Still, not her place to ask. Curiosity just might kill her though. At least she was on the right track. Now to fine-tune it. "Remove all references to Eric's love life."

There was a pause, then her hand dropped and started circling lightly on the same picture. She kept her eyes closed and could only hope that the stylus was doing as requested. A quick moment later, she opened her eyes to find the folder showing, but the label now held a series of weird marks on it. She didn't know what it had done.

She thought about Eric's life and was relieved to see him as a child and in several other stages of his life, even as an adult.

Using her sketchbook, she fanned herself to cool off, finding it hard to remove the images she'd seen so briefly. Her attraction for Eric stemmed from a lot of different things. He was unusual, which was part of it. He also felt comfortable, easy to talk to. He had a sense of confidence that was very attractive.

She'd never considered it before. She'd wondered about sex a lot, had experimented some with Jeff. Then he'd moved away. She was an idiot thinking about sex at a time like this. Eric might perish in the war going on his world, and if he survived, his own father might kill him. She sat up straight again. She'd returned to her world. That meant the death sentence on Eric's head was in effect.

A groan escaped her. That so wasn't good. Why hadn't she thought of it before leaving him alone? Why was it that for every step forward she made, she ended up further back? It's what she didn't know that got her. Like her parents and their religion. Not quite believing she was planning on changing something she'd wished for ages, she realized it had to be their choice, not hers. Closing her eyes, she asked the stylus to reverse the changes she'd made to her parents' belief system. She didn't know what to say about her father's presence. Could she reverse that, too? And what if she didn't want to reverse it. Was that cheating?

Quickly deciding this wasn't something to fool with, she asked the stylus to reverse the changes she'd made unknowingly since this mess started. Hit the reset button, so to speak. Was there an undo function on this thing?

The stylus went to work. Then it stopped. The work was over so quickly she could only assume it was a minor fix in the fabric of things.

Or something beyond the scope of its abilities.

Had anything been fixed? Now wasn't the time to check, her parents would be asleep and she wasn't going to wake them. She needed to spend her time now learning what she could. She needed more information on the history of Eric's people and the Louers.

She settled into what had become a routine and let the stylus do its thing. This time she concentrated on gaining information so she was at least on equal footing with the others. A tiny niggle of worry bugged her. What had Eric said? Something about potential damage from crossing the veil. His people limited their research trips and monitored them closely. Was it for that reason they didn't travel back and forth on a whim?

Could this system of learning cause her physical harm? Was brain damage a consideration? Deliberately, she shut those thoughts down and replaced them with happy, healthy thoughts about how much smarter these sessions were helping her to become. And how harmless they were to her. She didn't know if it would work, but her parents' conversion had happened as a result of a random thought. She didn't dare take a chance.

A shiver went through the house.

She opened her eyes in shock and gulped hard. She hadn't done that, had she? Her hand rested on the side of the sketchbook like normal. The picture appeared to be of more file drawers, the information archives. What about the Louers? Please don't let that be them. She closed her eyes, "Stylus, did Louers cause that odd vibration?"

She read out the answer. "No."

Her shoulders slumped in relief. "Well, thank God for that," she whispered under her breath. Then it hit her. A realization that chased all other thoughts from her mind. This experience had been taken to a whole new level. She'd *asked* the question – instead of *writing* the question. She gulped, her mind racing forward. For all the weirdness, it would make communication so much easier.

Quickly, she asked if it had information on how to stop the Louers from entering her world and how to get them out of Eric's world.

Her hand never moved.

She turned to a clean page and concentrated hard on the same question. Once again, nothing. Panic set in. What if the stylus didn't have the answer?

Where were the answers coming from anyway? The archives of Eric's people. Maybe, their archives didn't have the solution to the problem. Several questions and much reading later, she finally understood. At the end of the war between the Toran and Louers a portal had opened, accidentally it seemed, and the scientists at the time had taken the opportunity to force the Louers through in an act of desperation. But her files contained more than just that general information. In truth, the Louers had been tricked into going through the portal. Eric's people hadn't even looked to see what was on the other side. They hadn't known if the Louers could even survive the crossing.

They hadn't cared. They were trying to get rid of a problem.

Therefore, the Louers had been exterminated.

She closed her eyes and shuddered. The Louers had suffered. She knew it. The archives hadn't been specific, but she'd seen those bony fingers coming through her living room. They were *not* normal looking. They'd been forced to adapt, evolve under extreme conditions. She read more. Originally a larger boned people, normal looking, they had been peaceful at first. Now they were a war mongering species.

Why though? Why had the Toran people had such a problem with the Louers? What could the Louers have done that was so bad? With her eyes closed, she searched further. A few minutes later, she opened them again, her gaze hardening in anger. The Louers had been slaves. They'd attempted a bid for their freedom and revolted. Banishment had been their punishment, at least for the few that survived. She hurt for them.

Were they only mindless animals intent on revenge? Could they even remember their origins? What were the chances of that?

She closed her eyes and asked her stylus if it had information on how to stop the current war going on in Eric's world. Still no response. Then she ran through a series of questions that touched on the same subject. Could the Louers be captured? Could they be sent back home again? Nothing she asked made the stylus move.

Finally, she picked it up and inspected the stylus, turning it over and over. Did it need batteries? Maybe it had quit working.

She pondered the tool again, and then asked it for information on how to save Eric. Her hand jumped back to the sketchbook to race across the page. Keeping her thoughts focused on Eric, she watched as a picture of her bedroom emerged. She understood. Eric wasn't safe over there. He'd be safe here. The good news was that her world appeared to be the safe zone. She asked the stylus if, with all the changes they'd made, the gates to Eric's world were still functional. Could the people leave?

Could she bring everyone over here?

The stylus glowed in her finger tips. The writing on the side shone in the darkness. Storey realized for all her new information floating around in her brain; she didn't know how to read this language. How could that be? Hadn't Eric been taught to read this language? Wasn't it part of their history? Or was it another ancient element lost to the ages?

She closed her eyes and asked the stylus for the information to understand the written word and symbols of its world.

It struggled with its movements, as if reluctant, but forced to answer. Was it truth bound? Not that she understood what that might mean. "Is there a reason not to teach me your language?"

The answer blazed in her mind. However, her hand wrote out the word *Yes.*

Wow. Direct contact. Almost beside herself with joy of discovery, she asked, "Why?"

It's dangerous.

"I'm making dangerous mistakes because I can't understand what I need to know. Isn't that more dangerous?"

So few of us know the language.

Us? She stared at it curiously before asking, "Are you a person?"

No.

"A consciousness?"

Yes.

Storey dropped the pencil and jumped to her feet. "I'm so stupid! Why didn't I try this earlier? Everything will be so different now." She paced the room in an attempt to calm down. It made so much more sense now. Finally, she stopped. There was so much more she needed to find out. She snatched up the stylus and her sketchbook. "Stylus – are you alive?"

No answer. She kept her hand on the sketchbook but there was no movement. Okay, so more questions.

"Can you think?"

Yes.

"See?"

No.

"Feel."

No.

She frowned. Had there been a bit of hesitation there? "Reason?"

Yes.

"Okay, that makes you a computer-like thingy. I can live with that."

It stayed quiet. Of course it did. But talking with it made it a lot easier to communicate on her end. It must have built in microphone equivalent. "Stylus, do you know how to preserve your world?"

Yes.

Relief swept over her. "That's great. How?"

Remove the threat.

"Yes. Exactly." She shifted to sitting cross legged again. "How do we do that?"

The stylus was quiet. She rephrased it. "Do you know how to do this?"

No.

"Does anyone?"

Yes.

"Who is that?"

Paxton.

"Paxton knows how to get rid of them?"

Yes.

"Where can I find him?"

In the lab.

Damn. How could they get in touch with him? "Can we communicate with him from here?"

Yes.

Storey's eyebrows shot up. "Really? How?"

I can communicate with his stylus.

"Of course. He'd have one too, wouldn't he? Okay, let's see if Paxton's stylus is responding, please."

There was a weird humming in the room. Storey scrunched her shoulders against data streams flowing into the air. This must be the way the Internet worked. That's exactly what she had right now – an intranet, like big companies had for their different offices to connect. Could the other styluses be reached too?

"Stylus, do your people know that you can talk to each other?"

No.

"Is this something you've kept secret?"

No.

"Are we causing any harm doing this?"

No.

She slumped back on her bed at that answer. Thank heavens for that. Ever mindful now about the consequences of her actions, she waited for the two styluses to talk. "Can I communicate with Paxton now?"

Yes.

Exasperated at the short answers and lack of instructions, she said, "How?"

Write the message and I will have the other stylus write the message in front of Paxton.

Story wrote, speaking out loud as the stylus formed the words, "Paxton, this is Storey talking to you from my world. According to my stylus, you know the way to stop the Louers. Please advise if there is something I can do to help. By the way, Eric took me to your world and then sent me back when we found your world under attack. Have you seen him? Is he safe?"

She waited a moment thinking about it. "Okay Stylus, send that message."

It went as you wrote it.

"Great. Every word?"

Yes.

"How will I know if he sees the message?"

His stylus has shown him already.

"Can you tell me his reaction?"

No.

"Of course not. That would mean understanding feelings, like shock. Horror, even." She pondered the situation. "Send him another message. Tell him he can write using his stylus and his stylus will send his message to my stylus, so I can read it." She waited another breathless minute then leaned forward. "Done?"

Done.

She waited chewing on her fingernails. "Damn it. Why doesn't he answer?"

He's answering.

"He is? Where? Oh." She turned the page and put the pencil to paper. Her hand jerked as the message flowed. She read it aloud. "Stay out of our world."

"Wow. After all that he tells me to butt out." What an ass. Her hand started moving again. *Eric is lost to us. Your fault.*

She gasped. "What? Eric's dead? No, that can't be." Hesitantly, she asked, "Stylus, is Eric dead?"

Her hand never moved. "I'll take that as a good sign." Paxton said lost to them. What did that mean?

"Stylus send another message, please. What does he mean 'Eric is lost to them'? Eric should have gone straight to the basement to meet up with them, as per the instructions he received while in his room." She waited anxiously, her pencil in hand. "Isn't he going to answer?"

He is.

There seemed to be a time lag of some kind before her hand started to jerk out the message. *Basement under attack. All thought to be lost.*

"Not possible. That was supposed to be the safe zone." What was that other place the guy said, Manshire? Mansfield? Mansfield, that was it. "Stylus send a message, please." She quickly wrote down her question about where this place was, who could have sent the message, and where was Paxton himself that he was safe?

It took a moment, and then her hand started writing. *Mansfield was the location of the portal used to banish the Louers. The global feed must have told Eric that and sent him to the basement. The basement was taken early this morning. There were so few people left. The others had been rounded up. Possibly being held in Mansfield. I'm in lab monitoring the situation.*

"Global feed? I don't think I want to know. And Paxton's in his lab? No, not possible. We were there this morning. How could we have missed him?"

She quickly answered him and asked why they hadn't seen him earlier.

His response was swift and sure. "None of my business," she read aloud. "Nice. Not."

He either didn't see us or didn't want us to see him. Either way, his behavior wasn't cool.

"According to the stylus," she wrote, "You know how to stop this war. I need to know how."

The response wasn't long in coming. *No, I don't.*

"Stylus, how is this possible?" Of course it didn't answer. "Okay, let me try that again. Stylus, is Paxton aware of his knowledge on how to stop the war?"

The stylus quickly etched out the word, *no.*

Okay, so he wasn't lying he just didn't know he knew. "Great. So Stylus, what does Paxton need to do to access this information?"

He needs to go into his memory banks and find the system used last time.

"But the system last time was an accident. He's not likely going to be able to recreate that accident."

No accident. Council project.

"So, like a secret government research project, huh? Figures, the archives say it was an accident. Well, we have a few of those going on here, too. Tell Paxton that, please."

Already done.

"Really? Wow, fast." She sighed and sat back to wait.

Her hand started moving right away.

How do you know about that? I can't remember those de-tails. Will have to access archive. No time.

Her hand continued to write, *The styluses are like old computers with long memory banks. Ask yours for the infor-mation. That's how I found out. My stylus answers questions. Yours will, too.*

She waited and waited. Nothing. She wanted to get up and storm around the room, but didn't dare do anything to stop the ongoing communications. "Why isn't he answering? Does he not know? Doesn't care? Or is he no longer there to care?"

After ten long minutes her hand started writing again. *Going to access archives. Eric had crossed into the basement. Triggered alarms with his signature. No idea what has hap-pened.*

"Can I go get him out?" Not that she was going to listen for his answers.

"Yes!" she read aloud. "Wow, what a surprise he actually gave me permission." She pondered a return to the other side. "Stylus? Will you remember this message in case I run into trouble from being in your world?"

Yes. All data is stored and transmitted.

"Yep. So, you are just like our computers. Only you use a pencil and paper instead of a keyboard. Cool." She hopped up and grabbed a thicker sweater out of her closet. It was her one chance to pick up anything extra. She'd yet to use the supplies in her bag, as it was.

The stylus in her hand started to vibrate. She raced over to the sketchbook.

Not quite like your computers. We were people once.
We were Louers.

CHAPTER 14

S HE CHOKED AND then choked again. "Did…did you say you used to be a Louer? As in you used to have a body and a mind?"

Yes.

"What happened?"

Slavery. Given to a research lab where I was bonded to the stylus to support the old man who'd been bonded to it for centuries before me. The risks were high. So, slaves were used to keep the soulbound objects functioning. The old man was failing and the bond had weakened. I don't know how, yet the next thing I knew, I was locked inside, joined as one with the previous souls. Soulbound.

Heat flushed upward then drained in hurry, leaving ice behind. Soulbound. Not bound to her soul, but a soul inside, bound to it. She shifted the stylus, to hold it almost reverently as she stretched out the fingers on her right hand. "Oh my God," she whispered. "I am so sorry. I had no idea."

Her left hand jerked under the impulses of the stylus. She quickly moved it to her right hand and let the words pour.

No. Most people don't. I haven't communicated with anyone in centuries. It feels odd. To feel anything is…unique.

She winced. "A good odd or not so good?"

A good odd. Rusty. Some of my capabilities are returning.

"Is that good?" She wondered what the hell she'd released.

Yes. There are many of us here. We have merged into one – the voice and mind of the same stylus. Each of us adds something, and the stylus grows in power. The older it is, the longer is has survived, the more of us are in here to keep it alive. The handler adds another element. In this case, you have increased our abilities tenfold. We thank you.

She gulped. "You're welcome. I think. I hope this is a good thing. Those people, Paxton, Eric and the others, aren't really open to progress. Not sure they'll appreciate this type of change."

No. Over time they will.

On that note, she turned around and finished packing her bags. "So, Stylus, how can we transport into the basement where Eric is? There are no gates there. I've never seen the inside, so drawing a door into it is going to be impossible and possibly not a good idea. Suggestions?"

The stylus was quiet. She laughed and picked it up off the bedding. Placing it on the sketchbook, she repeated, "I need a codex to travel around your world. Can we make one – is that possible?"

Possible – not practical. There exist many in Paxton's office.

"Paxton. Right. I can get to the lab." She pulled out the drawing she'd used with Eric the last time and ten minutes later she found herself back in the lab. And face to face with Paxton.

She grinned at him.

The color drained from his face. "What? How are you here?"

She wiggled the stylus in his direction. "It hasn't failed me yet. Are you aware that souls are bound to this stylus?"

She watched him straighten. "Or should I say whose *souls?* These are Louers. They were normal people, whose only wrong was wanting a better life for themselves – not one of servitude. The Torans kept them as slaves, as prisoners." Outrage stiffening her spine, she stalked toward him.

"I know what we did," he snapped. "I read the archives. That is ancient history. That we're paying for it today is unacceptable. We didn't force any of them to become bound to the stylus, they were volunteers. It offered them a chance to live forever. They were also well compensated for their sacrifice. We aren't monsters, you know."

"Then why banishment to another dimension?" She couldn't help feeling that something else must have been going on.

"How would I know?" His voice rose. "I'm old, but not that old. It wasn't during my lifetime."

She shook her head. This wasn't getting them anywhere. "Where were you earlier, when Eric and I were looking for you?"

He reared back. "I've been here all along."

With a shake of her finger, she said, "Nope, you weren't, because we searched for you. Even at your apartment."

His eyes widened. A faint blush rose as he swallowed. "I was in my apartment until I heard intruders. I hid, then raced back to my lab."

Storey's gaze widened in understanding. He'd been the one that had knocked over something in the living room. They'd just missed each other. It would be laughable if it weren't so frustrating. She refocused. "I need a codex and training to use one."

He pulled himself up to his full height and raised his nose into the air. "Absolutely not. There is no way. It will kill you."

Storey pursed her lips. Instinct drove her to pull the small blank notepad out of her pocket and slip the stylus into her fingers. "Stylus, will wearing a codex kill me?" The words formed on the page instantly. She lifted the book to show Paxton while reading it aloud. "No."

It would have taken a better person than she was to hide her triumphant look. Her grin widened. "Didn't know they could talk, did you?" She waggled the stylus in her fingers. "You don't know the first thing about them, do you?"

Paxton took a tentative step toward her, his eyes locked on the stylus. "How is it you have learned all of this in just a few days?"

She couldn't be sure, but he sounded slightly mollified instead of angry. She hadn't wanted to rub this in his face. "Because I didn't come at it with preconceived assumptions like you did." She thought that was a reasonable answer. From the glacial look fired in her direction he didn't agree. Adults and their egos. They made life so difficult.

"So yes or no on the codex? I am willing to go and get Eric; however, I can't get to him without a codex – unless you'd like to come to unlock the doors?"

He shook his head widely, white tufts of hair flying in all directions. "No, no. I can't leave. I'm needed here."

"Then you have no choice." She held out her arm.

"These aren't toys. Extensive training is required to use these. You can't just put one on and expect to be a pro."

"I don't expect to. Show me the basics so I can get to Eric. We can use *his* codex from there. Can't you sync one codex to find his codex?"

Paxton's brows drew together in surprise. "Yes. Yes, I can." He busied himself at a desk piled high with metal pieces while she waited. She glanced down at the stylus and paper. "Do you know how to work the codex, Stylus?"

Her hand jerked immediately. *Much of it.*

"Good. Maybe, we'll do well after all."

Paxton raced toward her. "Here's a simpler version. We use these for visitors." He strapped the smaller unit on her wrist while firing instructions on its functionality.

She turned her arm slightly, admiring the look. "This is way cool." And it was. She could use something like this on her own world. Not that he'd appreciate hearing that. Still, when this was over…nope, not going to happen, the FBI would never let her keep it.

"Now pay attention. I'm punching in the identity code of Eric's codex right now. As soon as I press this last button, you're going to arrive at his side. That could put you into many horrible scenarios. This codex can't save you." As if the force of his stare could infuse common sense into her, he upped the wattage and directed it into her eyes.

She blinked and pulled back slightly. "No, but my brains and my stylus might."

He snorted. "And they might not. This is war. People are dying. You might, too."

That stopped her in her place. "I wanted to ask you about that. What is the population of your city here? Millions, thousands or only hundreds?"

"Thousands here and millions over the planet. We don't have your overpopulation problem."

"Thousands only? Are there children here?"

Paxton reared back. "Of course. We have a natural order of things. Children here do not run amuck, like in your world."

"What's the average life expectancy here?"

His lips thinned. "We live much longer than you do. I don't want your people coming over here and treating us as lab rats to find out our secrets."

Understandable. Yet it was okay for them to do that to her? Not that they'd said so to her. She shook her head. "That's not my intention. What I was thinking about was that your people are extremely long lived, so death is an even greater loss here. With your peaceful life, you're also not used to the trauma of war, of living in fear every day."

"And you are?"

"Not personally, but I've been raised with the possibility of a terrorist attack any day. We learn to live well in spite of it. That doesn't make us naive."

"My people are innocent."

"Good." She smiled and headed to the spot Paxton pointed out. She tucked her stylus into her jeans pocket, grimacing down at her clothing. At home she'd grabbed a sweater, but why hadn't she considered changing her jeans or socks and shoes? Too late now. She checked out her location and the circle she was standing in. "Here?"

"Yes. There. Return as soon as you can – with Eric."

She nodded and pushed the button. Having traveled by codex before gave her some warning as to what to expect. It happened so quickly though, she didn't have time to adjust. When the blackness cleared, she blinked and spun around.

The room was empty.

Surely not. Had the correct identity number been punched in? She had to believe in Paxton that much. Then where was Eric? She walked the small area, looking for some evidence that he'd been there.

A desk and several chairs sat in the center of the room, undisturbed. She bent to look underneath.

Something twinkled below. She pulled a chair back and reached for it.

Eric's codex.

Oh shit. She stood up and spun around, looking for where Eric could have gone. There was no sign of a fight. No disruption to the room. Just plain…nothing.

Weird. Where were the doors in this place? Hidden? Why was nothing ever easy on this side of the veil? She walked the room, dragging her fingers along the wall, looking for breaks to denote a door. There weren't any. She stared up at the ceiling. Nothing visible. The floor? It was covered in a deep red flooring that sat like a cross between tile and carpet. Unique. She studied it, wondering if there was some kind of level below. Did basement mean the same thing here as it did back home? She wished she could ask Paxton. She brightened. She could. She pulled out her stylus and sketchbook, muttering to herself as she wrote the note, "Paxton, the room is empty. No doors or windows. Only a table and chairs in the center of the room. No sign of anyone. Eric has lost his codex. It was on the floor under the table."

She waited for the stylus to show signs of an answer from Paxton.

Impatience gnawed at her. Finally her hand started moving. *Move the table. Door is opened by knocking on it. Eric couldn't have 'lost' the codex. He's been taken and either had it cut off or removed it himself.*

Not good. She walked over to the table and turned it to the right. A smooth, sliding noise sounded behind her. She spun around to find a large door had shifted to the side. It hadn't been discernible before. Hard to believe.

Standing in the doorway, she realized there was only a

dark black space beyond. Where were the damn light switches in this place? "Stylus, how do the lights turn on?" Even as she spoke the lights flashed on. Apparently they were voice controlled. She studied the long hallway now visible before her. A single closed door waited at the far end. She walked down and pushed it open. It led to another large room. This one was also empty. Not knowing what else to do, she returned to the room where she'd found his codex. "So, Stylus. Where is Eric?"

She expected a quick answer. Instead she got a weird humming sound. What was that? It almost seemed like her stylus was thinking things over.

I'm not registering him.

"Uh oh?" She stared at the pen. "What does that mean?"

It means I can't see his energy signature anywhere.

Her stomach knotted. "What? What does this mean?"

He is no longer in this dimension.

ERIC TRIED TO sit up. Bad idea. He gasped at the sledge-hammer in his head. Bile from his stomach climbed up the back of his throat. Then he felt his bare arm. His codex was gone. He vaguely remembered being grabbed and putting up a crazy fight before taking a direct hit on the side of his head. He could have lost it then. Or they'd taken it. Whoever 'they' were. The loss of the codex could also contribute to the headache. He groaned softly. Brutal.

"Eric? Are you awake?" A familiar voice spoke through the pounding in his brain.

Eric tried to open his eyes. Pain forced them closed again. "I'm here," he whispered to his father. "Where are we?"

"I don't know. I was hoping you might know."

Peering through slit eyes, Eric saw his father squatting down in front of him. "What happened, sir?"

Shifting to sit on his ample butt, his father said, "We had just finished the emergency Council meeting when the alarm sounded. Louers. Everywhere. Seemed like hundreds of them. I don't know how or why. They overran us in minutes. At least I think they're Louers. They look different, though. Not like they used to look."

"Different how? What did they used to look like?"

His father peered around nervously, whispering, "Like us. Exactly like us."

What? Eric shot him a startled look. He didn't ask the burning question he wanted to ask. Instead, he went for the one next in line. "What are they like now?" Moving gently, he struggled into a sitting position, heaving a sigh of relief when the room stopped spinning. The fear in his father's voice made him look up.

"Mutants. Deformed, weird looking things. Nothing normal about them now."

"That makes sense in a way. They've had to evolve to survive. Did you know what the place was like when your people banished them?"

"No and I don't care." Sitting like a rotund Buddha, his father placed his hands on his knees and glared at Eric. "They're killing anyone who resists and rounding up the survivors. We've been taken somewhere. I'm afraid it's off planet."

That stopped Eric in the act of trying to stand up. "As in across the veil?" Just then the smell hit him. He bent over, plugging his nose. He groaned. "What's that smell?"

"Louers. We're prisoners in the Louers' dimension."

Nasty. Experimenting, Eric unplugged his nose and shuddered at the rank aroma. All the archives spoke about a horrible smell at the gate. Words hadn't done it justice.

He struggled past it to refocus on the mess they were in. From Storey's history, he'd learned that every war sported winners and losers and the losers, historically, became prisoners. When able to cross dimensions, it wasn't hard to imagine returning the prisoners to your home. Particularly if you needed slaves.

"Are we being guarded? Has someone come to speak with you?"

"No." His father shook his head. "There's been no one."

"Does anyone have a codex?"

His father leaned closer to whisper, "I do. I don't know the coordinates to punch in."

Eric could take care of that. His father's unit wouldn't be strong enough to take everyone back at once. "Are they taking the codexes away?"

"Don't think so. We were herded forward as a group. Outside of giving us a quick check, they haven't done a massive search. There's one codex and even a couple of taprins,"

"Good." But not great. The simple taprins were basic codexes but wouldn't have the power and functionality to help out here. There wasn't a weapon amongst them. Why would there be? Until now, there'd been no need. "Slip me your codex. I can get out and back with reinforcements in no time."

His father glared. "Not without me. If you're going, then so am I."

Eric grimaced. "It's best if we all go at once. The guards could come any moment." He studied their surroundings and the ragged group surrounding them. "How many of us are here, about twenty?"

"Closer to thirty."

"Marshal the others into a group. I know where to go." Eric accepted his father's codex, clipped it on, then punched in the coordinates for Stanshor mine. That would get them clear of here, then they could jump to another point. The mine was better for a large group like this. Paxton's lab could be the second jump. Not that it would help much unless it was secure.

"We'll try for the mine," he whispered to the group gathered around him. "Everyone squeeze in as close together as possible and hang on. We're trying to move a lot of people at once. I don't know that I can take everyone in one jump."

"You're not leaving me here," blustered a big man in the back, shoving the others in closer.

"Nor me." That was a young woman holding a young child.

"I ain't staying. No way. Those things are going to come back and I want to be long gone." An older man spoke, Eric vaguely remembered seeing him in the Council chambers.

Eric understood their feelings. "Who else has a codex?"

Two people held up their arms. "Darn." They were both simple versions. "Okay. Let's try."

He hit the button on his codex and waited for the sequence to run on both, picking up the signals of each other, building power in their connectiveness. Who knew if the codex worked in the Louers dimension? They could very well end up someplace else entirely. He figured anywhere had to be better than here.

Reassuring blackness swirled around them. He closed his eyes and willed the portal to open. A wretched smell filled their nostrils and the air became fetid, hot. He coughed several times.

"Is it working?" whispered one of them.

The blackness deepened until Eric couldn't see his father's face in front of him. Isolation often accompanied a dimension journey, with the cold an ever-present symptom. He closed down inside and waited. Uneasiness knotted up his stomach. They had so few options. This had to work.

"Are we there yet?"

"No."

Another long minute of frightful silence. A child whimpered. Her mother hushed her. "Shhhh. We'll be there soon."

"Will we? I've never been in such a long transfer." The grumbler was in the back of the group. Probably the big man who'd spoken up earlier. Eric didn't have any guarantees to offer. "Some of the gates aren't working well. Not to mention with this many people the transfer will take twice as long."

Just when he thought they were trapped, the mist started to recede. Sighs of relief washed over him. The air lightened, the others grinned. He turned to look around. "We're here. Where ever here is?"

As the mists dissipated, Eric realized they weren't in Stanshor at all. He didn't know where they were.

"What is this place?" Everyone stepped back to look around. Curiosity and relief wreathed their faces. Trees, trees, and more trees surrounded them. Blue sky and sunshine looked down on them. Eric had to wonder if they'd crossed to Storey's world.

"I'm not sure yet. I don't recognize it."

"I don't care where it is. It's not with the Louers." A

murmur of agreement wafted through the crowd.

"I want to go home." The little girl huddled against her mother's legs.

Eric's father walked over to him hooked his arm and led him a little ways away. "Have you heard about this place before?"

Eric circled the area. "I don't think so." He walked a few steps further as his father watched. "It's possible we're in another dimension."

"You mean we've crossed the veil? That we might be in the human's dimension?" he hissed, staring around as if something might jump out at him. "Do you know how dangerous it is over here?"

Eric looked at him oddly. "Yeah, I think I do. I've been back and forth several times with Storey. Still…I'm not sure that's where we are."

"So how do we find out?" The self-elected group leader, the large, burly man who'd complained before, stepped forward. "Don't get me wrong, I'm glad to have gotten out of that place…where's home though?"

"Please keep in mind that the Louers have taken over our home. We don't want to jump back into the same situation. I'll contact Central and let them know we need assistance."

He tapped his codes, watching the colors shift in the right order. Reassured, he contacted Central next. No one answered. Sending off a message, he hoped someone there would see the flashing signal and hit the receiver. He didn't want to consider the possibility of no one being there to receive it. Using other codex functions, he tried to get a location for this place. The wrist unit beeped and flashed and in the end, came up with an error message.

Even the codex didn't know where they were.

Chapter 15

Storey stared at her stylus. "Eric is in the Louer's dimension?" He'd better not be. She didn't relish trying to find her way over there.

Her pencil jerked out an answer. Or somewhat of an answer. *Yes. No.*

She sighed. "Which is it?"

He was. He is no longer.

"How do you know?"

His father's codex has recently been recalibrated for Eric's use.

"Then where are they now?"

In another dimension.

"What other dimension?" Exasperation at the short answers and having to pull teeth to get information was draining her. "My home?"

Close.

"Close." She stopped puzzled. "There are only three dimensions here." After a moment, she added, "Right?"

Her pencil answered quickly. *There were only three, but now there is a fourth.*

"Oh no." She groaned and closed her eyes briefly. The onion. "You mean the one I created to make a safety net for my world? Is Eric caught in there?"

Yes.

"Which means I can't wipe out that dimension without wiping out Eric and his group?"

If you destroy the dimension, you will also destroy everything in it.

"Such as?" The stylus remained quiet. "Could we wipe out the Louer's dimension?"

Yes.

"Yes?" she questioned. "So that's one way to stop them. Wipe them out and everyone in it will disappear, too. Drastic but as a last resort…possible." Except how could she know who else might be over there at the time? If the Louers were taking prisoners, then they'd be destroyed as well – including Eric, if he went back to rescue his people.

"Can you talk to Eric's codex?"

The codex is a machine. It does not talk.

"Right." She knew that. "Can you program the codes on Eric's wrist to give him the coordinates to get back home?"

Yes.

"Then do so." She wanted to jump up and down. This would all soon be over. Eric would be home safe and sound. Paxton should be sorting through the archives for a way to get rid of the Louers and she could go home. She frowned. She might need to fix a few things there yet.

I put in the coordinates for Paxton's lab.

"Good. Let's head back and we should arrive in time to meet them." She studied her codex. Paxton had programmed the original destination, not a return trip. The plan had been to use Eric's codex to get home. "Stylus, can you send the coordinates of Paxton's lab to my simple codex? Paxton didn't program a return trip for us."

Done.

Thank heavens for that. Now to get back and stop this

solo act. She punched the button she'd used last time and the wrist unit went off in a series of flashes and beeps. The black mist rolled around her, bundling her in a tight tornado of swirling black. She closed her eyes, hating the sense of isolation this type of travel created. One could get lost in the mists.

A shudder rippled down her spine. Lost in-between. Not a nice thought.

The mists started thinning. She relaxed, closed her eyes. It would be over soon. Several minutes later, she opened them and frowned. "Why isn't this over?" Frustration and the beginning tendrils of fear twisted in her stomach.

She waited. The mists still surrounded her, but seemed maybe less thick? Or maybe that was her imagination. The weird black gate they'd used when re-entering Eric's world popped into her mind. That had had a similar feel.

Her uneasiness grew. Following her instincts. "Stylus, have we arrived?"

She could barely see the writing on the page, even when held up to her nose.

No.

"Damn." Something had gone wrong. How to fix it? What would happen if she stepped out of the mist? She'd most likely be torn to bits. She shifted her weight from foot to foot. Another few minutes went by and she checked her wrist codex again. The lights continued to flash with bright colors. Who knew what that meant? "Stylus, can we contact Eric in any way?"

The stylus hummed. *Not at the moment.*

"Can we contact anyone? What about Paxton?"

More humming. *Yes.*

"Explain the situation to him, please." He should know

what to do.

The humming intensified then shut off sharply. *Communication has been disrupted.*

"Damn it. I can't just stand here in the middle of a transition. What can I do?"

No answer. Her stylus never moved.

She groaned at the silence. "What's the use of being able to communicate if you can't help me problem-solve?" More silence. The stylus, like any computer, could only answer direct queries. "Okay. Stylus, can I get out of the middle of this gate?"

Yes.

She brightened. "How?"

Time.

She snorted. "That's something I don't have." Just then the mist started to darken again. She spun around, terrified. "What's happening?"

The blackness deepened into a morass of seething energy unlike anything she'd ever seen before. It had taken on a powerful, negative feel. She cried out. "Stop. Stop. What's happening?"

The energy spun faster and faster. She screamed as the pressure in her ears built. She crouched down, covering her head with her arms. Pain ripped through her mind.

She collapsed to the ground.

"PAXTON!" ERIC GRINNED at his aged mentor. His disreputable looking group gathered around him, relief and joy on everyone's faces.

"Eric, Councilman. You made it." Paxton raced toward him, joy beaming across his tired face. "I'm so glad to see you are well."

The strain of the last twenty-four hours had taken its toll on the older man. His hair stood out in all directions. For the first time in Eric's memory, Paxton's robes were dirty.

"What's the status at Central?" asked his father, his massive bulk collapsing onto one of the many chairs.

"We're not sure. So far, you're the only ones I've seen. Except for Storey, that is. Communication's down everywhere." Paxton lowered his face into his hands and rubbed his cheeks.

"Storey? Did you say Storey was here?" Eric couldn't believe it. Fear and joy warred in his heart. She was supposed to be home safe, not caught up in this mess. "Where is she?"

"I thought you would know. She went to the basement to help you…then I received a garbled transmission a few minutes ago saying she was having trouble with the codex and needed help." He shook his head. "The transmission cut off."

"Where was she last?"

"We calibrated her taprin to arrive at your side, based on your codex. Only we didn't know it was lost. I tracked her until communications went down," he pointed to one of his monitors. "My stylus received only part of it."

Eric looked at him quizzically. "Your stylus?"

Paxton glared at him. "That little girl is too smart. She not only figured out how to use her stylus, but she also found out that the styluses can communicate with each other."

Eric's jaw dropped.

The Councilman leaned forward in shock. "What? An otherworlder discovered things about our way of life – our tools – that we didn't even know? How is that possible?"

Paxton faced him. "I'm not sure. She seems to have a very inquisitive mind."

"That's not good. Not good at all."

Before the discussion got out of hand, Eric stepped in. "She had to figure out what the stylus could do on her own. When you have training, you're told what you can and can't do. We never questioned what we were told. She's had to constantly question and test the capabilities of the stylus in order to understand it."

His father's bulbous face darkened like a tomato. "You can't believe she is smarter than we are. That's not possible. We are far more brilliant than those…those animals," he blustered.

Excited murmurs wafted through the group.

One tall, spindly man half-stood. "Otherworlder?" He looked around at several of the others. "Are you saying there's a girl from the other side of the veil here? Here, in our dimension?"

Eric winced. He'd forgotten they had an audience.

"Not to worry. She'll be caught soon. And terminated. I have a standing kill order in effect for her actions."

Eric's hands fisted in sudden fury. "Right. Her actions. And what actions were those? To pick up what to her was nothing more than a pencil? To have it become soulbound to her without her knowledge or permission? For that you've put a death sentence on her head?"

Silence.

Everyone turned to look at the apoplectic councilman.

"Lies. All lies. The Louers attacked us because of her. She's behind everything ill that's befallen us." His father stood, his bulk so rounded and unsteady that Eric wondered if he'd topple over any moment.

"She is not. She didn't let them in. We snuck into her world and carelessly left the instrument over there. Do you realize we've put their entire world at risk with our actions? She picked the artifact up. That's it. She never did anything to us. She even offered to help solve *our* problem, and you ordered her to be put to death."

Eric couldn't stop the bottled bitterness that flowed with the unfairness of it all. "She came back to help us – even knowing there was a termination order on her head. The Louers went to her house. Did you know that?"

"And you know what else? She *stopped* them. That little schoolgirl from the other side of the veil stopped the Louers from entering her home and her world. We should be thanking her, giving her an honored place for her bravery. But no, you set the guards after her. Ordered me to retrieve her, so you could dispose of her here. You're being blind and foolish in trying to wipe out the one person that could actually save us." His voice roared across the room, stunning everyone into silence.

Paxton moved first. Racing to Eric's side, he laid a hand on his shoulder. "Easy, Eric. I don't think that the Councilman understood the situation."

Eric shrugged off his hand. His bitterness came out in full swing. "Oh he knew. In his all-knowing arrogance, he even ordered my death – the death of his only son – should I fail to return her to face her sentence."

The murmuring moved from person to person in a growing wave of unrest. They faced the Councilman in collective outrage. "We have a visitor from the other side and you want to kill her? Are you trying to start a war with those people, too?" The big burly spokesman settled into a wide stance, his hands fisted. His face reddened in anger. "Am I to understand, we sent a team over to this little girl's world and left a soulbound item behind?"

Someone else called out, "How is that possible? Where's the soul it was bound to?"

The Councilman's red face swelled with temper. Eric watched him struggle for control. His father was a born politician, meaning a born liar. His father's face smoothed over and he beamed at them, then proceeded to answer their questions. "The person who owned the stylus fell seriously ill on his research trip to the other side. He was rushed back here before the team knew that it had been lost. We believe that the veil, combined with the severity of the owner's illness, weakened the stylus's bond. Since then it's been trying to come back home, using this young person as its vehicle."

A woman who'd been quiet up until now stepped forward, her little daughter clinging tightly to her hand. "Has she done anything to hurt us?"

"No." Eric jumped in before his father could. He faced the group, looking each person in the eye, trying to explain. "She's an innocent in this. We don't know if she had anything to do with the timing of the Louer attack, that's possible, but she's not responsible for this war. Even more importantly, a Louer entered her dimension by ripping through a wall in her house and I watched her banish him to the far reaches." He turned to face his father. "She came to help us do the same thing."

His father, the esteemed Councilman, snickered. "She came to help *you*. What is she, another of your disreputable friends?"

Eric's blood pounded at the insult. His father had never approved of his friends. Any of them. He'd gone out of his way to separate Eric from everyone. Thankfully, his father had never learned of his one and only girlfriend…ex-girlfriend. His jaw clenched. It gratified him to see his father backing up a step. Fighting for control, Eric finally managed to speak a moment later. "Of course you would put her down like this. She's never treated you with anything but respect, so I think you could accord her the same. I would be honored to count her as a friend. She has many qualities that I admire. Not the least of which is stepping in to lend a hand, even when her own life is threatened."

"That sentence can't be still in place," protested the woman. "That's hardly fair."

"No, it's not fair. Except my father, the Councilman, never rescinds an order. Even if it's wrong." His bitterness resonated throughout the room. He winced. He hadn't meant to let everyone know how deep this went. But then he'd spent a lifetime trying to live up to his father's expecta-tions, even though he knew there was no way he ever could succeed. The dam had to break sometime. "It doesn't matter. I'll go find her and send her home again."

"Now wait. That's not right either," blustered the burly man again. "We need her."

The mother shook her head. "Not if it's going to cost her life."

The burly man turned on her so fast, she stumbled while trying to back up. She snatched her daughter up into her arms. "Why not?" he said. "Our lives are at stake now, too. Or do you want to go back into that black hole again?"

"That's enough." Paxton entered the fray. "Eric, regard-less of her future, she's in trouble if she hasn't made it back yet."

"Right. Then it's back to the basement for me."

"No. She's left there. She's caught somewhere in transit."

"How's that?" Eric's heart hitched. With all the chaos around them, anything could have happened to her. Damn he wished she was here, safe and sound.

"According to the monitors, she left the basement over half an hour ago. She should have been here within minutes. I can only think with all the disturbances that codex travel is messed up. I have no idea where she is."

The young women stepped up. "Can't you contact her? There must be some way to reach her."

Paxton stared down at his stylus frowning. "She got her stylus to communicate with mine somehow." He turned his over a couple of times. "I've been soulbound to mine for over a century and never knew. Then, maybe mine can't. Stylus, can you talk?"

Silence.

He shrugged. "I didn't think so."

"How did she communicate with you?" Eric stepped up and stared at Paxton's stylus. "Did they communicate to each other?"

"Yes, except her stylus contacted mine. I don't know how to get mine to initiate a conversation."

Eric ran over to the desk and pulled up a stylus tablet. Holding it out to Paxton, he said, "Write down the question."

"This is foolish," he protested, but did as asked. His stylus made an odd scratching sound as he wrote, requesting it to contact the other stylus. "There." He glared at Eric, holding up the tablet for everyone to see. "Now what?"

"If she can answer, your stylus will receive a message."

Paxton snorted. "I doubt it. This stylus has been used in the same way for a long time. It's not going to open up communication just because I request it."

"No, yet it did at the request of her stylus, correct?"

"Which isn't going to help right–" His hand jerked. He gasped. Eric grabbed Paxton's hand and placed it on the tablet. The stylus immediately started to write.

"Lost." Eric read it out loud.

Paxton read out the last half. "Need help."

A gasp rose through the crowd. "How do we help her?"

"Stylus, can you get the coordinates of the other stylus?"

The stylus wrote down the word *yes*. Paxton's eyes bugged out. He spluttered, "This is impossible. You can't just talk to it. It's not alive."

"Why? It's your belief system that needs to shift here." Eric didn't care if Paxton was uncomfortable with this or not. "Stylus, please write down the coordinates so that I can key mine to match."

Instantly a series of numbers showed up on the tablet under Paxton's astonished gaze. "There, see? Now…" Eric ignored him and punched in the numbers. "Considering that the codexes are whacked right now, I can only try. Let's hope I can reach her."

He stared at Paxton. "Then again, if you come with me, I'll be able to communicate with her no matter where I end up."

Paxton shook his head vigorously. "No, I can't do any more codex travel. Go. If it doesn't work, we'll figure something else out."

The options weren't great.

"Back in five, I hope." He walked over to the port and hit the button.

CHAPTER 16

S TOREY ROCKED BACK and forth, her stylus in hand, sketchpad resting on her crossed legs. A chill had set in, forcing her to drag her sweater out of her backpack to stay warm. She'd tried to exit this mist on foot, in her mind, and through her pictures. So far nothing had worked. She turned to yet another clean page. At this rate she would run out of paper. Just the thought of it sent her flipping the book and writing on the back of the previous page. "Now what? Stylus, do you have any idea of how to get us home again?"

No.

She retried the same question as she had for the last ten minutes. "Can we communicate with anyone?"

A humming again. Well that had to be progress. "Who?" she asked, the words bursting free before the stylus had a chance to answer.

Eric.

She brightened. Yay, something had shifted. And for the good. Straightening her back she asked, "What do I need to do?"

Nothing.

What? "Is he coming here?"

"Storey? Are you there?"

Eric. She jumped to her feet. "Eric! I'm over here. Follow the sound of my voice." She kept talking, loudly. Inside relief spilled over to fill her right down to her toes. She was saved.

"I'm coming. Keep talking." His voice sounded like it was right next to her, that she could reach out and touch him. A hand reached through the mist and brushed her arm. She shrieked. Then a face. Eric.

She launched herself into his arms. "Oh, thank God. Am I glad to see you. I couldn't go anywhere. I don't know what happened." She was babbling and couldn't seem to stop herself.

"Shhh. It's okay. I'm here now. You're safe. The codexes are gimpy from the rips in the veil. Let's see if we can get you out of here." He tried to back out of the mist. He could move through, yet the minute she tried, it wouldn't let her pass.

"Weird. The mist thinks it's taking you somewhere. It won't release you."

"That doesn't make any sense."

"No it doesn't. Still, it goes along with everything being wonky right now."

"Can we cancel it?"

He reached for her armband and frowned. "You've just got a simple Codex. That's no good."

"Wait." She reached into her back pack and pulled out his codex. "I have yours, too."

His face lit up. "Great. Then I can take off my father's." He exchanged the codexes. "Mine is a controller. I should be able to clear the codes frozen on your unit." Drawing his brows together, he punched a series of buttons before tapping in a series of numbers.

Storey couldn't help but grin at the familiar musical notes. Such a teenager thing to do. Just hearing something normal again made her feel giddy with relief. "I like your ring tones."

"Ring tones?" He glanced up briefly, confusion clouding his eyes. "What do you mean?"

"Like the cell phones in my world. Yours plays music when you use it."

With a shake of his head he went back to studying the unit on her arm. "Sorta. Each is a code though."

"Whatever." She didn't care if it played movies, as long as it got her out of here.

"There. Now when I code into the coordinates for the lab, the mist should disappear."

A few tense minutes after the sounds stopped, the blackness lightened.

"It's working," she cried out.

She threw herself into his arms again. Reaching up, she planted an enthusiastic kiss on his lips. As she pulled back, she realized what she'd done. "Sorry."

"Sorry for what?" he said, his voice husky and soft, his arms wrapped tightly around her. "There's not a man alive that would object to being kissed by a beautiful woman."

A delicate shudder worked down her spine, pooling in her belly.

"Are you all right?" He pulled back slightly to peer deep into her eyes, forcing her to close hers or let him see how much he'd affected her.

She burrowed deeper, mumbling, "Yes. Yes, I'm fine. Just cold."

He tugged her back into his arms, letting the heat of his body warm her up. "This should help. The mist is always cold."

Snuggled in tight, Storey couldn't help wishing that they

could stay like this a little longer. "Good. I'm so glad you found me. I was running out of options," she admitted against his chest.

He nudged her chin up so he could look her in the eyes. "It wouldn't have happened if you'd stayed home. What possessed you to come back? You knew it would be bad."

"Yes." Then she remembered. Explaining how she'd learned to communicate with the stylus and how it had given the knowledge necessary to protect her world from the Louers, she added, "I think it might be the answer here, too."

He gave her a quick squeeze. "Paxton doesn't like that you can do more with yours than he can with his."

She grinned. "They can talk to each other. They were Louers once."

"What?" He moved her back slightly and gave her a little shake. "What did you say?"

It took a moment to repeat what she'd learned from her stylus. "According to Paxton, they were volunteers, except I'm not sure how much was really voluntary when compared to the promise of a better life than slavery. There are several souls bonded to my stylus, so it's no longer one person but a compilation of many souls together. After so long they've fused together as one unit."

"But Louers? They're our hated enemies."

She took a few steps back and lifted her stylus and whipped out her pocket notebook. "Says who?" she scoffed. "Stylus, were you an enemy of Eric's people?"

Her hand jerked. She held it up to him to see.

"No?" He looked at her doubtfully, and she realized he thought she'd written that answer herself.

"Were you perceived as their enemy, Stylus?"

Yes.

"Were you enslaved to them?"

"Yes," she read to him, holding up the stylus triumphantly. "See. They were Louers."

He stared at her. "How did they get from being slaves to this nightmare they've become today?"

"Stylus can you answer that question?"

Her hand immediately went to work. *The Torans believed Louers were trying to rise up against them. They banished us. In the process, we fought back and tried to take some of our old owners as slaves.*

Figures. History repeated itself, regardless of which side of the veil humanity inhabited.

"That's regrettable if it's true, yet how does it help us now?"

"I don't know, except all information is power." She turned around. "The mist is gone. Can we leave now?"

"Yes." He focused on his codex and tapped in new codes. Once again musical notes accompanied the flash of numbers and colors.

Please let it take us where we want to go this time.

Black snaked up her legs.

She stepped closer. "I hate this part."

"It should work this time."

"Should?" Was that squeak her voice? She barely held back a shudder.

"Like I said, we've been having trouble with the codex travel."

"You said that?" She didn't remember that. Everything else had disappeared from her mind in the excitement of seeing him. Storey closed her eyes at the brief vertigo that always accompanied the transition. Within seconds, the mist thinned before pooling at the bottom of their feet.

Paxton's lab.

"Oh, thank heavens for that." Her breath rushed out in a whoosh, only to be sucked back in shock. The room was full of people.

Staring at her.

"Uh, hello."

Smiling tentatively, she studied them. Tired, dirty and very happy, they appeared relaxed. What a weird combination, especially given the war going on. They smiled back. At least they were friendly. Her gaze wandered around the familiar room and froze at the sight of Eric's rotund father glaring at her. No, that was too light a word. Animosity oozed from him.

Storey glowered back. *Asshole.*

As much as she hated it, she couldn't stop her back from stiffening or the sense of vulnerability creeping in.

Would he order her to be hauled off to the dungeons? Or had the kill order been rescinded? She'd forgotten to ask Eric.

"Easy," whispered Eric. "This isn't the time"

"As long as he wants me dead, it is."

"There is some doubt about the sentence, in light of your actions." Paxton rushed to assure her.

Storey studied his features, realizing how much the current situation had aged him. She grimaced. "Nice thought, but excuse me if I don't believe you."

"Don't blame you. Not sure I do either," Eric muttered beside her.

He placed a hand in the small of her back and nudged her forward. "Give me the codex. It's not going to do you any good." Taking it from her, he walked over to Paxton and handed it over. "This is the broken unit."

"The energy tears will be the root of the problem." Paxton examined it, turning it over several times. "But I might be able to fix the unit."

"It's not worth it." Eric pulled his father's codex out of the backpack. He handed it over to Paxton as well, then turned to address his father. "Not sure this unit is in working order, either. Might need to be overhauled as well."

Storey watched anger blitz across Eric's father's face. The Councilman was not happy. She couldn't help warning Eric. "Uh oh. He's not happy with you," she whispered.

Eric glanced down at her in surprise, then studied the anger and frustration on his father's face.

"Is this her?" a tiny voice piped up, interrupting the conversation.

Storey turned toward the sound to see a waif peering around a tall thin woman. Storey grinned. They did have children here. And females. She'd started to wonder where the hell they were or if this was a male only society. "Hi, who are you?"

"Sammy?" A smile peeked out, followed by a tinkle of a laugh.

"Well, hello, Sammy. My name is Storey."

"Hi." She ducked behind the woman's leg again.

Storey wanted to bend down and talk with her, but a robust male stepped in, blocking her view. With his arms akimbo and jaw squared, she realized that not all of these people were open to her presence. Storey smiled. "Beautiful child."

"Hmmm." His eyes narrowed, studying her.

She lifted an eyebrow in question, keeping a relaxed smile on her face. Eric put an arm around her shoulders. "Everyone, this is Storey. She is from the other side of the veil."

Storey shot him an amazed glance. "You told them?"

"Yeah, that whole secretive thing wasn't doing it for me. Besides, I figured honesty might be the better approach, considering we're trying to lift the death sentence on your head."

"Yeah. How's that working out?"

"Half and half."

She shook her head. "Nice. Now that Paxton knows how to stop the Louers, maybe I could go home."

"What?" Everyone turned to look at Paxton.

He shook his head. "No. No, I don't know how to stop them."

"According to the stylus, you do."

"Well, the stylus is wrong," he snapped. "How did you stop them in your world?"

"I erased them." She grinned at the dumbfounded looks staring at her. Eric smirked at her side. "And when I went back last time, I added another dimension between the Louers and my world. Don't know how well that's working out though. It's a touchy thing making changes on a large scale. Some unexpected things happen."

"Dare I ask?"

She shot Eric a look and shook her head "No, let's just say I might have to fix a few things when I go back." What were her parents thinking about now? Wiccan, Catholic or maybe by now, they've converted to some no-name cult. Or had everything reverted to normal and her father was gone from her life again? She groaned softly. Just because she'd instructed her stylus to reverse all unintentional changes didn't mean it had. Or that the attempt had worked. Only time would tell.

"Erased?" Paxton's voice squeaked between them. "How is that possible?"

"With the stylus." At the puzzled look, she added, "The Louers ripped through the veil and tried to enter through my living room wall while Eric and I were there."

Several of the women in the crowd gasped and held their children close. She couldn't blame them.

The big man's thick busy brows beetled together. "Is that the first time they've made it to your world?"

She nodded. "I think so, but I don't know. I imagine they came through in that spot because it's almost the same place as the portal I accidentally created in the beginning."

Understanding lit up Eric's face. "Right. You jumped through the floor. And they came in at nearly the same place where you'd have disappeared." He patted her on her shoulder. "That's the first time I got that. Wow. That makes so much sense. So, when you erased that Louer, did you also erase the crossing?"

"No, I don't think so." She thought about it again. "Or I recreated it when I crossed over again."

"Hmmm."

Paxton lifted his hands and shook them in her face. "That won't work here. It's not possible."

Storey studied his anxious features. "I don't know about that. To make it work, I'd have to either remove every tear except one and shepherd them back throughout that hole and erase it afterwards."

Eric shook his head. "Hang on here. Let's go back to that creating a new dimension. How did you do that? And what's to stop them from crossing from that dimension into yours?"

"As I don't know what they're capable of, I can't say that

they can't. Keep in mind they haven't before. And consider that that they may not want to for a couple of reasons. To start with, this dimension is a copy of our world, the world they left behind. It's nice and they might be happy there. And second, they may think that this new world *is* my world. After all, who'd be there to tell them the difference? Third, they won't know there are other dimensions to go looking for. Why would they? Their current world isn't very pleasant, is it?"

"No." Paxton shook his head. "It's a dark, damp place with only a few hours of light each day."

"Nice." She grimaced. "No wonder they mutated into something so different from the slaves you once had. You could try to understand them before slaughtering them."

Eric's father stomped to his feet. "That's enough. What do you know of our world? You come here and cause trouble, yet still come out smelling like royalty. You're not. You don't belong here. You don't belong with my son."

Storey turned to face him. His beady eyes glowed with hate. She lifted her chin. "No, I don't. I have my own world to go back to." She refused to let this man intimidate her after all she'd been through already. They had no idea.

"Then go home and don't ever come back," the Councilman snapped.

She snorted. "Would love to. Not sure I can, considering that the tears in the veils are making travel very iffy right now." That didn't mean she couldn't travel by drawing though. Not that she was ready to tell him that. They still hadn't solved the Louer problem.

Paxton nodded his head. "That's quite right. Quite right, indeed." He wrung his hands and shuffled his feet. "She can't travel now."

"So fix it. That's your job. Take care of it. Then ship her home. Today." The Councilman settled back and crossed his arms over his ample stomach.

Storey's heart, always willing to forgive, hardened. He was an asshole. She opened her mouth to give him a piece of her mind when Eric's hand squeezed her shoulder. "Steady," he whispered before turning back to face his mentor. "Paxton, any idea of how long it could take?"

Paxton shook his head vigorously. "Oh dear. I don't know. I just don't know. I can't fix the tears with the Louers travelling back and forth."

"So we have to stop the Louers first?"

"Right." His head bobbed up and down. "I think so."

Storey glanced over at Eric to find him studying her, a questioning look in his eyes. "I can't deal with them all. Not this way."

"I know. The problem, as I see it, is the lack of information. There's no way to know how many have crossed into our world or how many more might come in a second wave."

"We don't want that to happen. This has to be sorted out and fast."

A weird sound ripped through the air. Storey backed up. Her stomach dropped. She knew that sound. It ripped through the room again. The crowd of people, sprawled across the floor, just starting to relax, jumped to their feet and cowered in a tight group.

"They're coming! Save us!" Hysteria erupted and the group scattered, with some people trying to hide under the tables and chairs. Eric's father jumped to his feet and raced to the door. "Save me."

Storey snorted. "Figures."

The Councilman glared at her. "It's their duty. My life supersedes theirs." He turned to glare at Eric, still standing at her side. "Eric, take me to a safe place."

The ripping sound sliced through the room. Storey jumped at the noise and spun around. She couldn't see the Louers, yet past experience told her it wouldn't take them long to break through the last barriers. She wondered how many there were in existence. Paxton wouldn't know and the Louer population could have changed drastically over the centuries, regardless of how many had been originally banished.

The others screamed and crouched lower. Mothers huddled protectively over their children. Storey took out her sketchbook and stylus. She couldn't afford to hide. Besides, there was no place left. She sat down in her favorite position on the floor and opened to a clean page. She'd need a new sketch book soon. Could she use the back side of her drawings or would that mix two together and create something she really didn't want to see? Best to not try for now.

Eric crouched at her side. "What are you doing?"

"I'm getting ready," she whispered nodding in the direction of the ceiling over the monitors. "They're coming in over there."

She spoke softly. "Stylus. I need your help. The Louers will be here any moment. How can I stop them from entering this room?"

Seal it.

She grinned. "Perfect. Let's do it." She put the stylus to paper and studied the picture slashing down at double speed. Her stylus raced across the paper, stopped, scribbled in place before continuing at a pace so fast she couldn't discern the lines as they appeared as part of the picture.

She tried to watch, but the frenzy of movement was just too hard to follow. Just like that, her hand stopped. She shook out her arm as she studied the image in front of her.

Eric leaned over her shoulder. The picture showed Paxton's lab, the full essence of the space down in a few strokes. A plastic layer appeared to cover the entire space.

"Sealant?" She laughed. Looking up she caught the panicked look on everyone's face. She bent her head. "Hey, Stylus. How about sealing each Louer and sending them back to their own space."

Too many.

"Hmmm. This world is also too large to seal, correct?"

Correct.

She rambled ideas aloud. "So how can we seal the space or the Louers? If we could do that, could we send them home any easier?"

Eric shifted his position to sitting on the floor. "You do realize you're sitting here in a life and death situation and talking aloud to a pencil?"

Casting a quick glance around, she realized her actions weren't exactly confidence building. "Eric, I have to toss out questions and see what rises for answers. The stylus isn't good at offering information. It answers my questions, though. Think of this as a brainstorming session."

He nodded. "Go for it."

Shooting him a quick smile of thanks, she returned to talking to the stylus. "Is there a way to put a tracking number or something similar on each Louer so that we can move them home as if sent by computer or codex?" She wasn't making any sense. She knew that, yet somewhere in there had to be an idea, a starting point.

"What are you thinking?" Eric frowned.

"I'm trying to figure out a way to track them all and then send them home before sealing the door, somehow forever. Then open a door to their new world. That's presuming they don't have technology that allows them to return here. And presuming that they like their new world enough to not to want to try to return here. Can we put a codex on each one and send them back or something similar? Obviously not that, as it would give them our technology."

"We can't go and catch them all in order to do that."

"Maybe we don't have to." She asked the stylus, "Stylus, can we do something like that?"

No.

"Okay. I can't just erase them one by one. I can't seal every room one at a time. There has to be something more global."

"Like what?"

"The stylus can track each one," she stared at her pen. "Stylus, that's correct isn't it?"

Yes.

Storey nodded. "Eric, do you have a way to move sup-plies across dimensions? Or large items from one spot to another? Like supplies to another city?"

He pursed his lips. "Yes, we can. We place codes on the items and send them through the gates, using codexes to set the destination." He studied her face. "Where are you going with this?"

Excitement bubbled through her. "Now we're getting somewhere. Why can't we can track them, slap on codes and ship them home? The next issue is how to subdue them? And how do we stop more from coming over?"

Paxton interrupted their musing. "I can fix the field so they won't be able to come across without getting injured.

They might try it once or twice, but by the time they figure it out I could have the tears fixed."

Eric stood up, stretched then squatted beside her. "That could take a long time."

"I know. I was hoping more people would have styluses and could help. Either that or have Paxton's stylus give us all locations and teams can go out at the same time. I doubt there are more than a dozen here at one time."

There were fifty in the first sweep. Her stylus moved freer on its own.

"How many are still here?"

One dead, seven wounded and taken home. Two escorted the injured home. Forty left on this side.

"Forty isn't so bad." She winced. Just forty opportunities to be captured or killed.

"I want to help." The burly man from the group stood up. "She's created a safe place for everyone, so they can stay here while we go hunting. I want to do my part."

"And me."

"I'm helping, too."

Before they realized what had happened, all the males in the group had stepped forward. Eric studied them. "Are any of you trained for codex use?"

"I'm in the reserves," said one of the younger men.

"I still think this is a bad idea," protested Paxton, facing the group. "You have no weapons, and they are bigger and stronger and meaner. None of you know what you're doing."

"Has anyone got a better idea? Do you have an army here? Security forces?" She asked the room in general. "We need to solve this ourselves before they return in greater numbers, now that they know how minimal your defenses are. Paxton, with the help of your stylus, can you organize teams to rescue your people from the Louer's dimension? If we can get them together in groups and send over teams with codexes, you could take them home very quickly. We need to make sure the Torans are here and the Louers are back on their side. Then we should be able to seal the tears while opening up the dimension in-between."

Frustrated, Eric ran his hand down over his face. "We're going to have to coordinate this very carefully. It could be dangerous. Storey, I don't want you in the middle of this."

Sadly she looked into his dear face. When and how had he become so important? So special to her? "I already am," she said simply. "Any of us could die on this mission, including you. There's no choice. The window of opportunity is now. Their numbers are down. Paxton might be able to reduce the numbers crossing over but if their numbers grow, there won't be any stopping them."

"She's right. If we're going, let's get a move on."

Eric looked around. "Two trained in codexes? No more?"

"Send one over to retrieve your people. Make sure more codexes are taken over there. Let the men who are prisoners use them. You'll move people much faster that way," Storey said.

Eric glanced over at his father, as if considering his participation, then shook his head. Storey agreed. The man had to have some redeeming qualities. He was the leader of Eric's people after all. It seemed to be her that brought out the worst in him. And once he'd slid down into that level, well…he seemed to revel in it. Maybe they could make peace when this was over.

"Fine. Two codexes, then two teams. One to do retrievals and pull in more men and the other to start dealing with the Louers until more teams can come to help."

"Right. Can we find a way to speed up the process? I won't know how long things are going to take until we get started. Paxton is needed here, otherwise I'd say take his codex as well."

"What about his stylus?" The same burly man took several steps toward Paxton, who backed up ahead of him.

"That won't work, his is soulbound, too." She lifted her stylus. "Can you give us coordinates right now for several Louers, a small group? Preferably in close proximity to where we are now?"

A distinct, deep humming filled the air. Several women ducked even though Storey tried to reassure them all was well. "It's my stylus. He's locating the Louers."

Her hand jerked, and the message appeared as if by magic. *There are nine Louers approaching the Center.*

"Nine in one bunch. A bit many?" She bit her lip, then shook her head. "The location means we need to take them first before they take over the rest of the building." Storey stood up and walked over to Eric. "I think we should go as a group and see how we fare. Four of us against nine of them is completely doable, particularly if we have the element of surprise," she added with a grin.

Eric looked at the eager faces around them and gave in. "It's almost a quarter of them. Not exactly a small group. We'd be better off going for a couple at a time."

Paxton shook his head. "No time."

"Right." Eric shrugged. "We'll give this a try and evaluate after this test group."

"Stylus, do the Louers have guns?"

No.

"Where is the best place to capture them?"

In the basement.

"Except that's where they caught all of us." Eric stood with his hands fisted on his hips.

"True. Where and how, Stylus?" Humming picked up as the stylus computed information. In the meantime, Storey checked over her backpack, making sure she was as prepared as possible.

In the anteroom of the outside entrance to the basement. They will enter there.

"Eric, do you have weapons to use?"

"Some."

"Stun guns? Tranquilizers? Something along those lines? You keep saying how advanced you are, so what do you have?"

"We *are* more advanced," Paxton spluttered.

Exasperated, she said "Then you should be able to subdue these things before we even see them. Don't you have gas you can put into this small anteroom? For that matter, you should have the ability to pipe gas into the ante room without us ever venturing near." She turned to the Councilman. "You run this place. Do you have defensive measures in place?"

He stared at her, disdainful fury marring his pudgy face. "No. Why? We've never needed anything like that before. We don't live in your society where you make war on each other all the time. We've never worried about our safety until you came here."

Storey groaned. "Not that again. You know what the problem is with your world? You're all talkers with no action. You'd talk yourselves to death if given a chance – at least that way you wouldn't have to worry about the Louers finishing you off."

She snatched up her bag off the floor. "I'm going down to the basement to do what I can to slap codes on these nine. Then we can ship them back where they came from. Either come with me and help or stay here on your fat butt and do nothing like you always do."

She strode to the door, pulling her small notepad from her pocket. "Stylus. Directions please."

Go through the door and turn left.

"Wait," cried out one of the women, "What about the sealant on this room? If you go out it'll break the seal and we'll be vulnerable again."

Hmmm. As much as she had no use for the Councilman, the women and children didn't deserve a life of servitude with the Louers. "Stylus, can it be resealed?"

No.

"Can we leave without disturbing the seal by using codexes?"

Yes.

She spun around searching for Eric. "Eric, are you ready?"

"Yes, just checking the status of the armory."

"How come you have an armory if you don't need such a thing," she asked mockingly of Eric's father. That pompous windbag really pissed her off. She wouldn't mind if he was captured again. It's not like he was doing anything to help save his people.

Eric shot her a sideways look. "Because at one point in time, we did need it. Therefore, for a long time we kept the training and weapons current. Then the threat died off and well…" He shrugged. "That could be a problem too. The weapons might be there, but I'm not sure what condition they are in." He motioned to the other men. "We'll go there first."

"Then let's move or we'll be too late."

He walked over, that wide cocky grin back on his face. Reaching out for her arm, he nodded to the others. "I'm dialing now. Step over."

The group rushed over in time for the black air to swirl around their feet and block out the rest of the room.

About damn time. This place would crumble with old age before anyone got down to business.

"Still as impatient as ever, I see," murmured Eric beside her.

She bent her head to hide her grin. If he only knew.

Chapter 17

A T THE BASEMENT, they split up. Eric took several men and headed to the armory. Storey and the remaining two men headed for the anteroom. She didn't know what they could do on their own, but hoped something would come to her on the way. The burly man strode at her side. The younger, pimple-faced, barely adult male loped along on the side. The teen smiled at her. She smiled back. "What's your name?"

"Horath."

She raised her eyebrow, "That's an interesting name."

He straightened, even his smile brightened.

"My name is Jendron." The burly man grinned knowingly at her. "Neither of us is mated."

What that had to do with anything, she didn't know. She knew enough to keep her mouth shut though.

She was grateful to see Eric ahead of them at the entrance to the anteroom. His nostrils flared. He lifted his head, almost sniffing the air. "They're here already."

"Good," she murmured. "Let's get in there and take them down."

He looked at her sideways. "How?"

"With the gun you're carrying."

His face broke into a half smile. "You've got that right. We have three stun guns. Old but still functional, I hope.

Still, we'll be lucky if we shoot four or five. What about the others?"

Storey smiled and tapped her sketchbook. "I'm not without some resources."

"True. But it takes time to draw. You aren't going to have that time."

"No," she said. "I won't. Maybe you'll be able to handle them all and I won't need it." She didn't bother telling him she'd been working on an idea. She opened her sketchbook, stared at it and started drawing. She created the same door that started this whole mess from her bedroom. She fell into the project with the same intensity she put into all her drawings.

She barely noticed when Eric set up position and motioned to the others to be ready. One hand on the doorknob, he turned back to Storey. "Are you ready Storey? In three, two, one…"

Storey raised her head and watched. Her hand, stylus gripped tight in her fingers, sketched at a mad pace. The gate was almost done, the latch, the shading. Just another minute. She watched the men even as her hand, the stylus clenched tight, drew at a furious pace.

Eric reached for the knob. He kicked the door wide and jumped in low. Storey peered into the room. Darkness, complete and utterly blinding, greeted them. There should have been some light from the windows, at least. Nothing. All her instincts screamed at her.

"What's wrong?"

He cast Storey a frown and nudged her to silence. Pulling his weapon forward, he entered the darkness. One step. Two steps. All he could hear was heavy breathing from those trying to peer into the room from behind him. A bright light flashed. He blinked, then blinked again. Black smoke wafted at the floor level.

The smell hit him first. Sour and cloying, the fetid aroma filled his nostrils and threw him off stride. He bent slightly, gasping for air. The black smoke thickened. Then it hit him. He scrambled backwards. It was a portal.

"Watch out," he yelled in warning. "It's an active portal."

"I made it. Toss them through." Storey screamed back. "I didn't expect it to be that big."

There was a shocked silence. Several of the men turned to stare at her, disbelief twisting their features. Eric, his temper barely held in check, said, "Next time, how about a little warning first, please."

"Sorry." She hunkered down close to the floor. Not a good start.

Louers rushed through the charcoal fog. "Don't let them grab you. They'll be able to take you through to their world."

Storey scurried further back from the action, shaking so bad her legs couldn't hold her. Panic knotted her stomach down tight. She grabbed her stylus. She'd drawn the portal, but hadn't expected it to be so big or right in the front of the door. Making the best of the situation, sketching as fast as she could, she placed a stickman in the room, labeled it Louer, then tossed him into the portal. A rasping scream sounded from the room. She ignored it, desperate to send another Louer into the portal. The intensity of the fighting increased and screams echoed down the empty basement.

The smell seeped out to where she was. It caught her sideways, making her gag. She choked several times, her eyes watering.

The sounds of fighting went on around her. She coughed a couple more times.

"Storey, a little help please!"

Crap, that was Eric. Still coughing, and with tears running down her cheeks, she returned to her drawing, urging the stylus to increase the speed. Another male screamed. Sounded like Horath. She sank deeper into her focus and sketched faster. The hell going on in there was beyond her experience. That Eric may not survive hadn't been a serious consideration before.

This hadn't been real before.

Just then Jendron tumbled out of the room to roll to a stop at her feet. He groaned and lay there gasping in pain. Scratches raked from shoulder to elbow on both arms as if he'd been grabbed and had pulled free. She thought he might be seriously injured, when suddenly he let out a roar, bolted to his feet and blasted back into the center of the fight.

Gulping hard, Storey tore her gaze away from the fighting and tried to draw. Her nerves rattled making it hard to hold the stylus. Consumed with panic, she had to close her eyes to stay focused. Imagining Louers attacking Eric, she mentally picked them up and tossed them in, her hand mimicking her action on paper. It was as if she could see everyone clearly in the melee. Eric was there, so was Jendron at the back. Sketch, pick up, and toss. Repeat. Suddenly she realized that Eric was in the air and flying toward the portal.

"No," she screamed. She scribbled over the portal and Eric hit the closed wall – hard. She'd shut the portal. Shocked, everyone stilled and stared as they worked to catch their breath. Only two Loures remained. Eric bounced to his feet and shot them both. Stunned, they collapsed to the ground.

"Oh, thank God." Storey clambered to her feet and raced over to Eric, throwing herself into his arms. "You're safe."

He wrapped her up tight in his embrace, his chest heaving from exertion. "Thanks to you."

Rearing back slightly, she noted, "Yeah. Apparently as I become more bonded to the stylus, my abilities or the scope of my capabilities is improving."

"No, really." He grinned and leaned over to kiss her, hard. Just as she was enjoying the feel of his mouth on hers, he set her aside. Laughing at the look on her face, he grabbed her hand and walked a few steps to stare down at the unconscious enemies. "Now what do we do?"

The others shook their heads and walked around the two prisoners. Sweat now mingled with the noxious odor of the captives. Raw sewage couldn't have smelt worse. Storey looked from them to the attack party. At first glance, everyone appeared to be alive and accounted for, although Horath held his arm at a funny angle. The others appeared bloody, yet not seriously injured.

Storey stared down at the creatures she'd yet to see up close. Her throat seized. Lord, they were ugly. Nothing she'd care to see late at night, that's for sure. They had human features, but were disproportionate in size. And hairy. She could only see the face of one, but it resembled the pictures she'd seen in natural history class of early Neanderthals, with huge foreheads and thick jaws. Their palms were thick and ending in impossibly long skinny fingers. She took a step back. She couldn't stand to be so close, their very skin reeked.

"How do you attach codes to send your supplies where

you need them?"

"We attach tags generated by the codexes."

"Will that work in this case?" She grabbed her sketch-book and asked the stylus to give her the sequence of numbers that the codex computer could pick up. Instantly, a series of numbers came up on the paper. "Okay, here they are."

"Do we just write this on their skin?" she asked.

Yes, but use me to write on them. Then the computer will have my signature.

Storey bent down to the thick arm in front of her. "Then we'll do that now. I'm at the first one. Let's repeat the first number." Once she touched the stylus to the Louer's skin, the stylus scratched out a complex series of numbers on his skin. No blood or obvious tissue damage. Weird. It was almost like a temporary tattoo when she was done.

She walked over to the other Louer and repeated the process. Then she stepped back and looked over at Eric. "This is your part now. Send them home."

Eric nodded and punched his codex several times bring-ing out the musical notes she'd come to understand. "Paxton gave me the destination code that he'd found in the archives used for Mansfield. Let's hope that's still effective." Mist started to swirl about. "Get out, everyone. The mist will take whoever is touching it."

The room filled with darkness. When Storey didn't move fast enough, she was grabbed and dragged out. The other men had filed out in front of them. They shut the door and waited.

Eric and Storey stared at each other. "Is this going to work?"

"It should. We send supplies to your world that way."

"Interesting." Something to keep in mind.

After a few minutes, Eric opened the door slightly, then threw it wide open. He grinned at her. "You did it. The room's empty."

She stepped in to look for herself. Turning back, she beamed a wide grin to the others. "I did it? This was a team effort." She kissed her stylus. "That leaves what, about thirty-one or so others? Let's go."

First though, they sent Horath and his broken arm back to Paxton for treatment. Now one man short, they needed smaller groups of Louers to keep the odds in their favor.

Using the stylus, they found a group of five Louers. This time they transported to within ten feet of their location, caught them by surprise and had them unconscious in minutes. The stun gun worked wonders now that the men were accustomed to using them.

Storey stared down at them in shock. "I haven't adjusted to arriving, and they're already out cold. This is great." With Eric's help they completed the code writing on all five. Standing back, Storey watched as Eric shipped them back to their old world.

"What's the chance of the other Louers being taken just as easily?"

Eric shook his head. "Not."

She grimaced. "Yeah, I didn't think so. Let's hope Paxton has closed those tears." She consulted with the stylus. "No more new crossings," she announced. "Still, we have another twenty-six to do."

The stylus came up with two in a group, and they were dispatched to follow their countrymen in a similar fashion.

"Two is about right, given how tired we are." Jendron said, adding, "Especially with there only being three of us now."

Eric nodded, fatigue pulling on his features. "Let's tell Paxton. He might have organized more teams by now. We're going to spend hours more doing this, otherwise. Not sure we'll be able to last."

Paxton reported everyone busy in rescue missions and fighting. It would be at least another hour before he'd have a second team for them, but he could send a couple of spare men for now. Eric's response was jubilant. "That's going to double our numbers. That's huge for us."

Coordinates were quickly sent and almost as quickly two more men, both big and broad, arrived. Storey grinned. Talk about a cool way to travel.

Feeling stronger with better odds, Storey's group repeated the process with another group of two and then one of three.

Jendron said, "This system works better with small groups." He wiped his brow, his voice deepening. "I don't know how many more we're going to be able to do. Now we need to find more this size."

"The stylus is looking." She glanced over at Eric. "How about an update from Paxton again. More teams would be wonderful."

He nodded.

"According to the stylus, the last of them are heading our way." She groaned. "Oh no, apparently three more have joined that group. There are now twelve Louers approaching. And no answer from Paxton."

Silence.

"Let's stay together and get the job done." Jendron had proven to be a great sergeant in this war. He took orders well and stepped up every time.

"Agreed," the group cried out, flushed with their success. Tired but willing. You had to respect the foot soldier.

Just then her stylus moved. Triumphantly, she read off, "Paxton is sending another team to meet us at the last location."

Watching the relief wash over the men, Storey could see how important it was for this last encounter to go fast and simple. She didn't want to consider failure and all that implied in this case. They'd been lucky so far. Horath's arm, a few scrapes and lots of bruises, but it could have been so much worse.

Just one more round.

The other team joined right in, catching on to the workable system. The battle was short and intense, passing in a blur of men, screams, and action. Storey, huddled out of the way, hadn't even needed her sketchbook. The men handled this one all on their own.

When the last one slammed to the ground unconscious, she jumped to her feet cheering. Eric threw his arms around her and swung her off her feet. They stayed like that for a long moment, both laughing in joy. It was done.

Well almost done. Using the same methodical system as before, they dispatched the last of them back to their homeland.

When it was done, she realized there couldn't have been a more anticlimactic ending. She smiled, a large, smug grin of triumph.

She didn't hear a thing before she was grabbed from behind.

"Eric!"

A vicious grip slammed her face against a hairy chest of an oversized Louer. The force of the blow knocked her breath out. She fought to fill her lungs with air, the arm around her ribs squeezing her tight. Christ he was big. She struggled futilely against the iron grip. Black spots crept through her vision. Just when she thought it was all over, the steel band loosened, her world flipped and she was thrown over his shoulder like a sack of dog food.

"Eric. Help!" Pushing against her abductor's back, she raised her head to see Eric racing behind them. The rest of the men were bringing up the rear.

Shit. She'd lost her sketchbook. She still had the stylus, stuffed uselessly in her pocket for safe-keeping. Now it was pinned between her and this massive shoulder. Using her fists, she punched the heavily muscled back and kicked out wildly. Her kidnapper grunted once, but never slowed.

Eric came fast. She could almost see his eyes. She couldn't miss the blast of the stun gun. It slammed into her attacker's ribs along his side, narrowly avoiding her. He stumbled. Storey bounced as the ground raced up to meet her. The Louer regained his balance, shifted her on his shoulder and struggled forward. She could respect his power and determination, but damn it, she was getting whiplash from all the bouncing.

Eric got off another shot.

The Louer slammed to a halt and swayed in place. Then he did a perfect face-plant on the ground. Storey was thrown on her back, her head slamming down hard and the heavy weight of the Louer crushing against her.

"Storey?" Eric raced to her side, his fingers gently stroking the line of her cheek and chin. "Are you hurt?"

She groaned. "I'm fine. Or I would be if you could get this asshole off of me, please." She coughed, struggling for air under the deadweight. The men hauled the attacker off, letting fresh air pour into her lungs. Lying still, Storey shuddered in relief. They'd talked about death and dying earlier. But it hadn't really sunk in that she might actually get hurt. She didn't have any problem imagining it now. Reality sucked.

While she recuperated, the men dispatched the last of the invaders home.

Reaching out a hand, Eric helped her to her feet. He handed her the missing sketchbook. Touched, she realized one of the men had retrieved it for her.

"Trust you to make things difficult, just when it's all over." He dropped a kiss on her temple. "I'm sorry he got the drop on us. We thought we had them all."

"So did I." Glancing around at the men gathered, she said, "We need to get back to the lab and make sure those tears are closed and fast." She sighed. "Then I need to open a portal from their world to the new copy I created somehow." She had no idea how, but knew she could do it with the stylus's help.

"Paxton's almost done with the tears. By the time we get there, he will be. Then you can do your stuff and it will all be over."

Over. What did that mean? Her heart hiccupped.

It meant the Louers were gone.

It meant Eric's world was safe.

It meant she wasn't needed any longer.

It meant – it was time to go home.

CHAPTER 18

ALL THE WAY back to Paxton's lab and the resounding victorious welcome waiting for them, Storey had trouble dealing with the fact that it was all over. That this nightmare she'd been living for days had finally finished. So much excitement. So much panic. So many emotions had rushed through her constantly. And then everything stopped. The chaos was over. Resolved. The change so sudden…she found it hard to believe.

It didn't feel right after days of living on a roller coaster. Days of fearing for her life and Eric's, the ranger from a different dimension. Now he was safe. She was safe. Everyone in his dimension was safe.

The stylus, the odd pencil-computer thingy with souls bound inside that she'd found, had opened a portal between the Louers' old and new worlds. Only time would tell if they'd make good use of it. Her stylus assured her the Louers were exploring their new world already.

Paxton, Eric's mentor and senior council member to the Torans, had monitors that tracked any activity through the areas where the dimensional tears had been repaired until they could all be reinforced. The process would take a bit longer, but like he'd said to her, they were on it.

They were on it.

As in she wasn't needed any longer.

They'd even managed a decent conversation over the future of her stylus. Now that she knew more, she understood his reluctance to let her keep it. Then he also understood her unwillingness to die in order to give it back. A truce had been made letting her keep it until they could figure out how to separate it from her safely. She kept the fake one tucked away. Just in case Paxton decided not to be as reasonable as he currently appeared.

Instead of feeling euphoric, she felt odd, uncertain. Almost as if she expected, no wanted, more chaos. And that couldn't be right. She wasn't a masochist. Why the hell would she want more war?

Because there'd been a certain attraction to being someone respected, looked up to. Someone who'd had answers. Someone who'd learned to do something others hadn't. Her pride and self-confidence had definitely had a good time here.

And it was coming to an end.

God, she was becoming downright depressed.

Off on one side, she watched the party going on around her. It was a standing-room-only crowd. Where had all the people come from? There were some seriously beautiful women here tonight which just added to her depression. She was still wearing her old jeans and sneakers.

Even the usually formal and uptight Paxton had let loose. He'd danced and hugged his way through the crowd. With so many well-wishers, she'd hardly had a moment to herself, hence her attempt at a time-out.

Eric found her a few minutes later. He slung an arm around her and held her close. "Hey, what's wrong?"

She relaxed against his shoulder, thankful he'd joined her. She needed this – him. "Nothing." With a light laugh, she added, "I was just ready for a couple of minutes of peace."

"That makes sense." He snagged a stool and sat on it without disturbing her position. "Are you ready to go home?"

"In a way. Then again, I finally feel connected to everyone here. We've been through so much, it's hard to leave."

"It's not forever. I'll be able to come over and visit, and you'll be able to come back."

"Will you though?" If she were honest, the fear of never seeing him again was behind the sense of letdown she'd been feeling all night. With his world safe again, it was over. There was no reason for Eric and her to meet anymore, except wanting to be together. They had a relationship – she just couldn't decide what it was. But she wanted to see where it could go. And how could she do that if they lived in opposite worlds?

If long distance relationships were hard to keep, then cross–dimensional relationships would have to be impossible.

And given his father's disposition, she didn't think she'd be welcome over here anytime soon. Everyone else had been friendly though. Several people had stopped to thank her. Some had stopped to ask her questions about her world and how long she was staying.

She needed to go home. Who knew what she still might have to fix back home yet? She'd left things in a bit of mess. And undone. Like the note on the inscription of the stylus she'd hidden on her computer. Not that it mattered any more as she could just ask the stylus about the lettering. Later, when she got home and had time to delve into all the unanswered questions.

"You look like you've lost your best friend." He bent

closer to peer into her eyes. "Are you okay?"

"Yes." She gave him a reassuring smile, at least she thought it was. "I'm just sad."

"That's understandable. You've made some friends here. We appreciate all you've done. We might even be able to have you come over as a consultant on some projects."

"Really?" She brightened. "I figured I'd never be welcomed back – considering I had a death sentence on my head at one time."

"A fond memory of your visit." He snickered. "Even if they aren't interested in having you consult, I'll come visit you. I promise. There's no way I'm giving up our friendship."

She closed her eyes briefly. Then said with a lilt in her voice, "Boy, am I glad to hear that. I guess I was feeling a little blue, thinking I'd never see you again."

"Not going to happen." He stood up. "But I understand you need to go home. Did Paxton speak to you yet?"

"He apologized and thanked me." She smirked. "I think he's still a little miffed at me over the stylus stuff."

Eric laughed. "I wouldn't be surprised. He's been bonded with his for over a century. It can't be easy to be shown up by a young girl. Especially one not even from his world."

"I can understand that."

Eric pulled her upright and into his arms. He stared at her quietly for a long moment. His voice rumbled from his chest. "Thank you for coming back and helping us. I'm not sure we'd have survived without you."

"You would have, just in a different way." Storey nestled closer. "I couldn't see your world suffering when I'd figured out a way to help."

"And help you did. The Louers are gone forever and all

because of you."

She lifted her head to caution him. "We don't know they're gone for good. It's too early to say. Paxton still has some work to do there. He has to make sure the portals are permanently sealed. We also don't know which dimension the Louers ended up in – for sure. We *think* we do, but…"

"Paxton will sort it out. He's nothing if not dedicated." As if to calm her worries, Eric bent and kissed her gently, then with growing enthusiasm.

"Arrumph."

They broke apart to find Paxton standing in the doorway. "I think it's time. Everyone wants to say good-bye to Storey and watch her leave."

"Oh." She brushed her shirt down and walked over to where her backpack sat on the floor waiting for her. "I hadn't realized."

They walked back into Paxton's lab to find a line had formed. Most of the Torans hugged her or shook her hand. By the time she'd reached the end of the line, she could barely hold back the tears.

Paxton gave her a codex. "So you don't have to travel by drawing portals everywhere. We all saw the result of that effort!" There was mixed laughter from the crowd, but it was the warm look on Paxton's face that made her respond with a big grin.

When the laughter died down, Paxton added, "This is a guest codex. It's pre-coded for your home, my dear. Thank you for all you've done."

Tears collected in the corner of her eyes. Storey smiled mistily. She really was going to miss him. "You're welcome." Impulsively, she gave him a quick hug.

Eric walked her over to the portal that his people used

for travel and dropped a kiss on her cheek. "I'll pop over tomorrow to see how you're adjusting to being home again. Your mom has to be wondering where you've been all this time."

"True enough." Thinking about her mother brought her father to mind. Oh boy. What waited at home for her? Not daring to speak in case she broke into tears, she managed a brave smile. He reached over and hit the button on her wrist unit. The familiar musical notes sounded.

Storey straightened her back, determined to go out gracefully. Forced to sniffle back tears, she gave the crowd a quick wave good-bye. It had been a hell of a weekend. She'd miss these people. Definitely Eric and maybe even Paxton. With a final look around the room, she recognized Eric's father, the hated Councilman, standing in the far back corner, a malicious grin on his face. What was he up to? He looked way too happy for her comfort.

The black mist swirled up around her legs.

The Councilman gave her a wiggling fat sausage finger wave good-bye and opened his other hand so she could see what he held. Nestled deep in the rolls was a long thin object.

Her stylus.

The black swirling mist rose to her chest.

She gasped in shock.

It was too late to stop the portal.

His grin fattened.

The room disappeared into darkness. Panic threatened. Oh God. Was she going to die now? Could the esteemed Councilman have actually won? She closed her eyes, hating him and what he'd done. How could she contact Eric to let him know? Without her stylus she had no way to communicate with anyone here.

Just then the mists thinned and cleared.

She turned around. An oily darkness greeted her. The rank smell of death rose, overwhelming her senses. She wrinkled up her nose and coughed, then coughed again. "Oh God. I know that smell!"

Hearing something behind her, she spun around. A long meaty arm stretched through the darkness. White bony fingers reached for her.

Stay tuned for the sequel
***Deadly Designs, Book II* in this series**
Or enjoy a different series!

Author's Note

Thank you for reading Dangerous Designs! If you enjoyed my book, I'd appreciate it if you'd leave a review.

Dear reader,

I love to hear from readers, and you can contact me at my website: www.dalemayer.com or at my Facebook author page. To be informed of new releases and special offers, sign up for my newsletter or follow me on BookBub. And if you are interested in joining Dale Mayer's Reader Group, here is the Facebook sign up page.
http://geni.us/DaleMayerFBGroup

Cheers,
Dale Mayer

Gem Stone (A Gemma Stone Mystery)

A juvie kid trying to stay on the right path stumbles into trouble…

Gemma takes her camera everywhere. From juvie hall to a halfway home, the new hobby gives her a focus she'd never had before and… hope in a future. Until she takes pictures of something that could get her killed.

And not just her…after she and another juvie girl are chased by a stranger to the halfway home that same night, the other girl goes missing and Gemma knows she needs help. But who can she trust?

Not the authorities that's for sure. Trusting them is impossible for a girl with her damaged history, and besides, who cares about a troubled kid…especially when trouble just naturally seems to find her.

In Cassie's Corner

Faith and loyalty are tested as a young girl learns what it is to believe – in herself, in her friends, and in life after death.

Cassie's best friend, bad boy Todd, is gone. Gone as in dead. Gone as in he's now a ghost.

But she doesn't realize that when he wakes her in her bedroom and begs her not to believe what they say about him. It's not until the next day when her parents tell her about the accident that she learns the truth…

The police believe Todd was living up to the family name, drinking and driving and coming to a predictable end. It's up to her to find out the truth and clear his name.

Todd is shocked at his sudden change in circumstances…and angry. He struggles with his new ghostly reality, realizing all he's lost as he watches his brother build a relationship with Cassie as the two pair up to find out what really happened to him.

The truth isn't always pretty, and Cassie has to be stronger than ever before. Especially when the whole world seems to be against her.

About the Author

Dale Mayer is a *USA Today* best-selling author, best known for her SEALs military romances, her Psychic Visions series, and her Lovely Lethal Garden cozy series. Her contemporary romances are raw and full of passion and emotion (Broken But … Mending, Hathaway House series). Her thrillers will keep you guessing (Kate Morgan, By Death series), and her romantic comedies will keep you giggling (*It's a Dog's Life*, a stand-alone novella; and the Broken Protocols series, starring Charming Marvin, the cat).

Dale honors the stories that come to her—and some of them are crazy, break all the rules and cross multiple genres!

To go with her fiction, she also writes nonfiction in many different fields, with books available on résumé writing, companion gardening, and the US mortgage system. All her books are available in print and ebook format.

Connect with Dale Mayer Online

Dale's Website – www.dalemayer.com
Twitter – @DaleMayer
Facebook Page – geni.us/DaleMayerFBFanPage
Facebook Group – geni.us/DaleMayerFBGroup
BookBub – geni.us/DaleMayerBookbub
Instagram – geni.us/DaleMayerInstagram
Goodreads – geni.us/DaleMayerGoodreads
Newsletter – geni.us/DaleNews

Also by Dale Mayer

Published Adult Books:

Psychic Vision Series

Tuesday's Child

Hide'n Go Seek

Maddy's Floor

Garden of Sorrow

Knock, Knock…

Rare Find

Eyes to the Soul

Now You See Her

Shattered

Into the Abyss

Psychic Visions Books 1–3

Psychic Visions Books 4–6

Psychic Visions Books 7–9

By Death Series

Touched by Death – Part 1

Touched by Death – Part 2

Touched by Death – Parts 1&2

Haunted by Death

Chilled by Death

By Death Books 1–3

Second Chances...at Love Series

Second Chances – Part 1

Second Chances – Part 2

Second Chances – complete book (Parts 1 & 2)

Charmin Marvin Romantic Comedy Series

Broken Protocols

Broken Protocols 2

Broken Protocols 3

Broken Protocols 3.5

Broken Protocols 1-3

Broken and... Mending

Skin

Scars

Scales (of Justice)

Broken but... Mending 1-3

Glory

Genesis

Tori

Celeste

Glory Trilogy

Biker Blues

Biker Blues: Morgan, Part 1

Biker Blues: Morgan, Part 2

Biker Blues: Morgan, Part 3

Biker Baby Blues: Morgan, Part 4

Biker Blues: Morgan, Full Set

Biker Blues: Salvation, Part 1

Biker Blues: Salvation, Part 2

Biker Blues: Salvation, Part 3

Biker Blues: Salvation, Full Set

SEALs of Honor

Mason: SEALs of Honor, Book 1

Hawk: SEALs of Honor, Book 2

Dane: SEALs of Honor, Book 3

Swede: SEALs of Honor, Book 4

Shadow: SEALs of Honor, Book 5

Cooper: SEALs of Honor, Book 6

Markus: SEALs of Honor, Book 7

Evan: SEALs of Honor, Book 8

Mason's Wish: SEALs of Honor, Book 9

SEALs of Honor, Books 1–3

SEALs of Honor, Books 4–6

Collections

Dare to Be You…

Dare to Love…

Dare to be Strong…

RomanceX3

Standalone Novellas

It's a Dog's Life

Riana's Revenge

Published Young Adult Books:

Family Blood Ties Series

Vampire in Denial

Vampire in Distress

Vampire in Design

Vampire in Deceit

Vampire in Defiance

Vampire in Conflict

Vampire in Chaos

Vampire in Crisis

Vampire in Control

Vampire in Charge

Family Blood Ties Set 1–3

Family Blood Ties Set 1–5

Family Blood Ties Set 4–6

Family Blood Ties Set 7–9

Sian's Solution – A Family Blood Ties Short Story

Design series

Dangerous Designs

Deadly Designs

Darkest Designs

Design Series Trilogy

Standalone

In Cassie's Corner

Gem Stone (a Gemma Stone Mystery)

Time Thieves

Published Non-Fiction Books:

Career Essentials

Career Essentials: The Résumé

Career Essentials: The Cover Letter

Career Essentials: The Interview

Career Essentials: 3 in 1